~your name.

Makoto Shinkai

New York

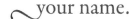

your name.

your name.
Makoto Shinkai

Translation by Taylor Engel
Cover art by Makoto Shinkai

©Makoto Shinkai © 2016 TOHO CO., LTD. / CoMix Wave Films Inc. / KADOKAWA CORPORATION / JR East Japan Marketing & Communications, Inc. / AMUSE INC. / voque ting co., ltd. / Lawson Entertainment, Inc.

English translation © 2017 by Yen Press, LLC

Yen On
150 West 30th Street, 19th Floor
New York, NY 10001

Visit us at yenpress.com
facebook.com/yenpress
twitter.com/yenpress
yenpress.tumblr.com
instagram.com/yenpress

First Yen On Edition: May 2017

Yen On is an imprint of Yen Press, LLC.
The Yen On name and logo are trademarks of Yen Press, LLC.

Library of Congress Cataloging-in-Publication Data
Names: Shinkai, Makoto, author, artist. | Engel, Taylor, translator.
Title: Your name / Makoto Shinkai ; translation by Taylor Engel ; cover art by Makoto Shinkai.
Description: First Yen On edition. | New York, NY : Yen On, 2017.
Identifiers: LCCN 2017003537 | ISBN 9780316471862 (hardback)
Subjects: | CYAC: Dreams—Fiction. | Sex role—Fiction. | Fate and fatalism—Fiction.
Classification: LCC PZ7.1.S5176 Yo 2017 | DDC [Fic]—dc23
LC record available at https://lccn.loc.gov/2017003537

ISBNs: 978-0-316-47186-2 (hardcover)
       978-0-316-47309-5 (ebook)

11

LSC-C

Printed in the United States of America

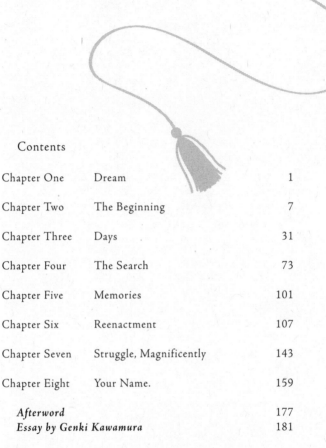

Contents

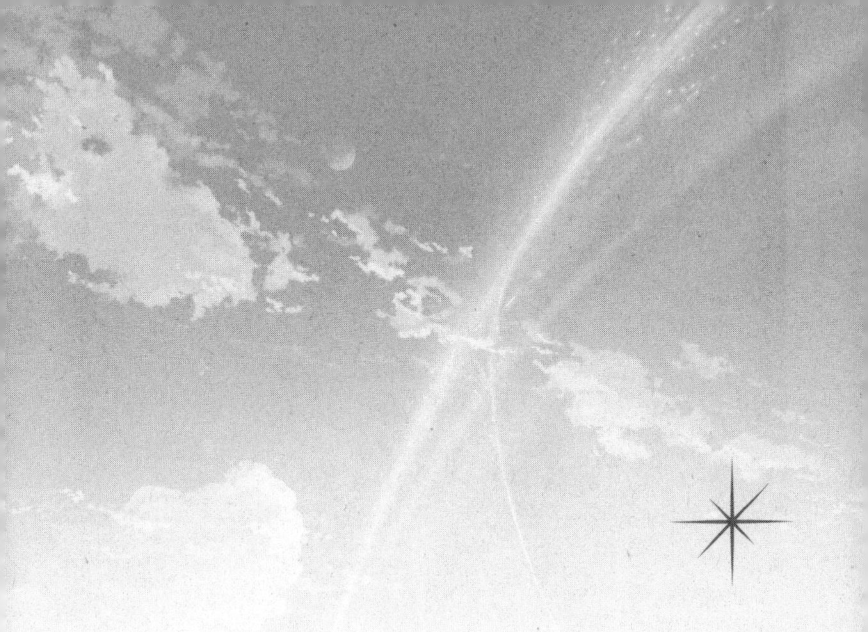

Chapter One

Dream

A nostalgic voice and scent. Cherished light and warmth.

I'm pressed against someone very special to me, so close that there's no space between us. We're bound to one another, almost inseparable. Like an infant cradled at its mother's breast, I'm wholly untouched by anxiety or loneliness. I've never encountered the sting of loss. A tingling, exquisitely sweet feeling fills me.

Abruptly, my eyes open.

There's the ceiling.

I'm in my room. It's morning.

I'm alone.

Tokyo.

…I see.

I've been dreaming. I sit up in bed.

In that two-second span, the sense of unity that enveloped me a moment earlier vanishes without a trace, without an echo. It's so sudden that, before I have time to so much as form a thought, the tears come.

Every so often when I wake up in the morning, for some reason, I'm crying.

…And I can never remember what I was dreaming about.

I wipe the tears away with my right hand, then stare at it. Little drops of water dot my index finger. Both the dream and the tears that briefly filled my eyes have already evaporated.

This hand once held something really precious…

I don't know.

I give up, get out of bed, leave my room, and head for the bathroom. Washing my face, I get the feeling that the taste and lukewarm temperature of this water once startled me, and I look into the mirror.

My reflection stares back. He seems vaguely unhappy.

Gazing into the mirror, I do my hair, pulling my arms through the sleeves of my spring suit.

I tie the necktie I've finally gotten used to, then put on my jacket.

I open the door of my apartment…

I shut the door to my condo. In front of me…

Tokyo's cityscape, which I've finally gotten accustomed to, spreads out before me. Just as I once learned the names of the mountain peaks, I can name a few of the skyscrapers now without even trying.

I get through the turnstile at the crowded station, take the escalator down…

I board a commuter train. Leaning against the door, I watch the scenery flow by. The city teems with people—in the windows of buildings, in cars, on pedestrian bridges.

A hazy, pale spring sky. A hundred people to a car, a thousand people to a train, a thousand trains crisscrossing the city.

*   *   *

Before I know it, just like always, as I gaze out over those streets...

I'm...
    ...looking for someone. Just one person.
I'm...

Chapter Two

The Beginning

I don't recognize that ringtone, I think drowsily.

An alarm? But I'm still sleepy. I was in the zone drawing last night and didn't get to bed until it was almost dawn.

"...ki... Taki."

Now somebody's calling my name. It's a girl's voice...... A girl?

"Taki, Taki."

Her voice is earnest, pleading, as if she's about to cry. A voice trembling with loneliness, like the glimmer of distant stars.

"Don't you remember me?" the voice asks me anxiously.

No, I don't know you.

Suddenly, the train stops, and the doors open. Oh, right—I was on a train. The moment I realize this, I'm standing in a packed train car. A pair of wide eyes hovers right in front of me. A girl in a uniform is staring straight at me, but the press of disembarking passengers is pushing her farther away.

"My name is Mitsuha!"

The girl shouts, undoing the cord she'd used to tie back her hair and holding it out to me. Without thinking, I reach for it. It's a vivid orange, like a thin ray of evening sun in the dim train. I shove my way into the crowd and grab that color tight.

＊　　＊　　＊

At that point, my eyes open.

The girl's voice—its echoes—still whispers in my ears.

…Her name is Mitsuha?

I don't know the name, and I don't know the girl. She looked really desperate somehow. Her eyes were brimming with tears. I'd never seen the style of uniform she was wearing. Her expression was serious, even grave, as if the fate of the universe rested in her hands.

Still, it was just a dream. It doesn't mean anything. By the time I think about it, I can't even remember her face. The echoes in my ears are already gone, too.

Even so.

Even so, my pulse is still racing abnormally fast. My chest is weirdly heavy. I'm sweaty all over. For the moment, I draw a deep breath.

Haaaah…

"…?"

Do I have a cold? My nose and throat feel funny. My airways are a little tighter than usual. My chest…really is weirdly heavy. How do I put this? Physically heavy. I look down at my body and see cleavage.

Cleavage.

"…?"

The soft mounds reflect the morning sun, and the pale, smooth skin gleams. A deep-blue shadow lies between the two breasts, like a lake.

Might as well squeeze 'em, I think, without missing a beat.

My hands gravitate toward them as naturally as an apple falling to the ground.

．．．．．．．．．．．．．．

．．．．．．．．．．．．

．．．．．．?

…!

The sensation blows my mind. *Whoa*, I think. *What is this?* I keep kneading earnestly. This is just… Wow… Girls' bodies are amazing…

"Sis? What're you doin'?"

I glance in the direction of the voice. There's a little girl standing there. She's just opened a sliding door. With my hands still pressed against my chest, I give her my honest impression.

"I was just thinking these feel way real… Huh?"

I look at the kid again. She's about ten, with twin ponytails and sharp eyes, and she looks like the sassy type.

"…'Sis'?" I ask the girl, pointing at myself.

So that means this is my kid sister? The girl looks thoroughly appalled.

"You still asleep or somethin'? It's. Break. Fast. Time! Hurry up!"

She slams the sliding door shut with a sharp *thwack*. *Fierce little girl*, I think, hauling myself off the futon. Come to think of it, I am hungry. Suddenly, a full-length mirror in the corner of my vision catches my eye. I walk a few steps across the tatami mats decorating the floor to stand in front of it. Letting my loose nightshirt slip off my shoulders and fall to the floor leaves me naked. I stare at my full-length reflection in the mirror.

Long black hair flows down my back, although it's sleep-tousled and sticking up in places. A small, round face holds big, curious eyes and lips that seem vaguely amused above a slim neck, deep collarbone, and a swelling bosom that seems to proclaim, *Why yes, thank you, I'm quite healthy!* Below are faint shadows of ribs, and then the soft curves of the waist.

I haven't seen one in the flesh yet, but this is definitely a girl's body.

…A girl?

I'm…a girl?

Abruptly, the drowsy fog enveloping my body is gone. My head clears instantly, then plunges into confusion.

I can't take it, and I scream.

∗   ∗   ∗

"Sis, you're so late!"

As I open the sliding door and step into the living room, Yotsuha's accusation flies to greet me.

"I'll fix breakfast tomorrow!" I say by way of apology.

This kid hasn't even lost all her baby teeth yet, but she seems convinced she's handling life better than her big sister. *I can't show weakness by apologizing!* I think, opening the rice cooker and scooping a gleaming white helping into my bowl. Whoops, is that too much? Well, never mind.

"Thanks for the food!"

I pour a generous dose of sauce over a smooth fried egg, pair it with rice, and put it in my mouth. Oh, yum. This just might be paradise… Hmm? I feel eyes trained on me, somewhere around my temple.

"So you're normal today, are you?"

"Huh?"

Gran is watching me steadily as I chew my food.

"She sure was somethin' else yesterday!" Yotsuha smirks at me. "Screamin' all of a sudden like that."

Screaming? Gran inspects me suspiciously, and Yotsuha grins (mocking me, I'm sure).

"Huh? What? What do you mean? What?!"

Seriously, what's the matter with them? It's creepy.

Ding-dong-ding-dooong.

Suddenly, the speaker over the door comes alive, deafeningly loud.

"Good morning, everyone."

The voice belongs to my friend Saya's big sister (currently employed by the Regional Life Information Section at the town hall). This place, Itomori, is a dinky little town with a population of fifteen hundred, so most people either know each other or at least know someone in common.

"Here are the morning announcements from Itomori."

The slow stream of words from the speaker is clipped into phrases. **"Here are...the morning announcements...from Itomori."** There are speakers outside, too, all over town, so the broadcast echoes off the mountains and overlaps with itself as if it's being sung in rounds.

Twice a day, morning and evening, this disaster-prevention radio broadcast plays throughout the town. Every house has a receiver to faithfully relay the daily announcements about local events: the schedule for the sports meet, how to contact whoever's in charge of shoveling the snow, yesterday's births, today's funerals.

"With regard to the Itomori mayoral election, which will take place on the twentieth of next month, the town election management committee has—"

Click.

The speaker over the lintel falls silent. Gran can't reach it herself, so she's pulled the plug. She's past eighty and wearing her usual traditional kimono, but even so, the gesture wordlessly conveys her anger. Even as I'm impressed by her chilly ire, I grab up the remote and turn on the TV without missing a beat. Picking up where Saya's sister left off, the smiling NHK news lady starts speaking.

"We're now just a month away from a visit by a comet that appears only once every twelve hundred years. For a few days, the comet is expected to be visible to the naked eye. With the celestial show of the century just around the corner, JAXA and research institutes worldwide are scrambling in preparation to study it."

There's a line of text on the screen—*Comet Tiamat visible to the naked eye next month*—and a blurry picture of a comet. Our conversation has lost its momentum, and the only noise comes from the three of us taking our meal and the NHK broadcast. Our soft *clink*s and *click*s sound a bit guilty, like whispered chatter during class.

"…Just make up with him already, wouldja?"

Out of nowhere, Yotsuha says something tactless.

"It's an adult problem," I snap at her.

That's right—this is an adult problem. Stupid election! Somewhere in the wind, a black kite gives a rather silly-sounding cry: *Piiihyororo.*

Saying bye to Gran in unison, Yotsuha and I head out the door.

The summer copper pheasants are crowing up a storm.

Traveling down the narrow paved path that runs along the hillside and descending several stone-walled stairways, we emerge from the shadow of the mountain into direct sunlight. Below us is a round lake, Itomori Lake. Its calm surface reflects the morning sun, glittering and glaring as though nobody's watching. The deep-green mountains form their ranks under white clouds in a blue sky, and a little girl with pigtails and a red school backpack skips along for no reason. Then there's me beside her, the dazzling, bare-legged high school girl. In my head, I try adding a grand string score to the scene as background music. Ooh, it's just like the opening of a Japanese film… In other words, we live in the boonies—very Japanese and a few decades behind the times.

"Miiitsuhaaa!"

After Yotsuha and I part ways in front of the elementary school, a voice calls out from behind me. It's Tesshi, pedaling his bike and looking cranky, with Saya seated primly on the bike rack and smiling.

"Hurry up and get off," Tesshi grumbles.

"I'm fine right here. Don't be stingy!"

"C'mon, you're heavy."

"And you're rude!"

This early in the morning, and they're already teasing each other like a married couple in a comedy skit.

"You two get along so well."

"We do not!" they chorus.

They deny it so earnestly it's funny, and I giggle. My mental soundtrack switches over to a jaunty guitar solo. The three of us have been friends for a good ten years—petite Saya, with her braids and straight-across bangs, and tall, skinny Tesshi with his burr cut and general lack of style. They always look like they're fighting, but given how their conversation is always perfectly synced, I secretly think they might make an excellent couple.

"Oh, Mitsuha, you did your hair properly today."

Saya, who's gotten off the bike, touches the area around my hair cord, grinning. My hair's fixed the same as always: two braids looped up and tied together in the back with the cord. My mom taught me how, a long time ago.

"Huh? What about my hair?"

Her comment sparks a recollection of the comments that sort of got lost in the shuffle at breakfast. I did it "properly" today—does that mean it was weird yesterday? As I'm trying to remember what happened, Tesshi leans in, looking concerned. "Hey, you did get your grandma to exorcise you, didn't you?"

"Exorcise?"

"Yeah, I swear you got yourself possessed by a fox!"

"...Excuse me?" I frown at the unexpected remark.

Saya speaks up for me, sounding disgusted. "Would you quit blamin' everythin' on the occult already?! Mitsuha's probably just stressed, that's all. Right?"

Stressed?

"Huh? Wait, hold it—what's all this about?"

Why is literally everybody worried about me? Yesterday was... I can't remember off the top of my head, but I'm pretty sure it was just a regular day.

…Hmm?

Wait, was it really? Yesterday, I…

"—And most importantly!"

A deep voice from a megaphone erases my questions.

On the other side of the road, with its rows of vinyl greenhouses, a little crowd of a dozen or so people is gathered in the ridiculously big municipal parking lot. Standing at its center, holding a microphone, is my dad, taller and bolder-looking than the rest. The banner he wears diagonally across his suit jacket proudly proclaims, *Incumbent—Toshiki Miyamizu*. He's stumping for the mayoral election.

"Most importantly, economic revitalization, in order to sustain the village restoration project! Only when we have made that a reality will we be able to establish a safe, worry-free community. As the incumbent, I intend to refine the community planning I've been involved with and see it through to completion! I will lead this region with new enthusiasm, creating a local society in which everyone—from our children to our senior citizens—can relax and enjoy fulfilling, active lives. I have renewed my resolve to make this vision my goal…"

It's such a skillful speech that it's almost overbearing. It leaves me cold—this campaign address sounds like it belongs on TV, not in a parking lot surrounded by fields. The whispers I hear from the crowd—*"You know it's gonna be Miyamizu again this term anyway," "It sounds like he's been spreadin' lots of cash around"*—make my mood even darker.

"Hey, Miyamizu."

"…Mornin'."

Wonderful. The greeting comes from three classmates I'm less than fond of. Even in high school, they're part of the flashy "in-crowd," and they snark at us—the "drones"—over every little thing.

"The mayor and the contractor," one of them says, shooting a deliberate glance at my orating father. When I follow suit, I see

Tesshi's dad standing next to mine, beaming. He's wearing a jacket from his construction company and an armband that says *Toshiki Miyamizu Supporter*.

The guy looks back at me, then at Tesshi, and continues. "Their kids are all buddy-buddy, too. Did your folks tell you to hang out together?"

This is so stupid. I don't even answer—I walk faster, trying to get out of there. Tesshi's expressionless. Only Saya looks bothered and a bit flustered.

"Mitsuha!"

Suddenly, a loud voice booms out. *Yeep!* My breath catches in my throat. I don't believe this. My dad lowered his mic midspeech to shout at me without the aid of electronic amplification. The whole crowd turns to look at me.

"Mitsuha, straighten up!"

I turn beet red. It's so unfair that I almost start crying. I want to run, but I desperately fight back the urge and stride away instead.

The crowd is whispering. "He's even tough on family."

"That's the mayor for you."

I hear my classmates snickering. "Ooh. Harsh."

"I kinda feel a little sorry for her."

This could not be worse.

The background music that was playing in my head a minute ago has disappeared, and I remember that this town, without a soundtrack, is an absolutely suffocating place.

With a sharp *tak, tak, tak*, the teacher writes a short poem on the blackboard.

Please don't ask me "Who goes there?"
I'm waiting here for my love, in the
September dew.

"*Tasokare*, 'who goes there?' This is the origin of the term *tasogare*, or twilight. You know the word *twilight*, don't you?"

Speaking in a clear voice, our teacher, Miss Yuki, writes **Tasokare** in big letters on the blackboard.

"It's evening, not quite day or night. It's a window when outlines blur, making it hard to tell who people are. When you might meet something that isn't human. It's a time when people encounter demons or the dead, and it has another name that reflects this. They say, though, that even before that, it had other names."

Miss Yuki writes the two terms on the board, but it looks like she's just shuffling around the same letters.

"'Scuse me, teacher! Question! What about *half-light*?"

Somebody speaks up, and I think, *Yeah, that's right.* I know *twilight*, of course, but the word I've heard people use to mean *evening* ever since I was little is *half-light*. When Miss Yuki hears this, she smiles gently. You know, our classics teacher is much too pretty to be teaching at a country high school like this.

"I expect that's local dialect, isn't it? I hear the elderly people in Itomori still use ancient Japanese words here and there."

"'Cause this here's the sticks," proclaims one of the boys, and people start giggling. He's not wrong. Sometimes Gran uses words that make me want to ask her what language she's speaking. Some of her expressions were abandoned by most of the rest of Japan a couple of centuries back. Idly pondering, I flip through my notebook, and then—on a page that should be blank—I see something written in big letters:

Who are you?

…Huh?

What is this? The sounds around me fade and grow distant, as if being absorbed by the unfamiliar handwriting. That's not mine.

I haven't lent my notebook to anybody, either. What? "Who am I?" What's that supposed to mean?

"…zu. You're next, Miss Miyamizu!"

"Oh! Yes'm!" I stand up hastily.

"Begin reading on page ninety-eight, please," Miss Yuki tells me. Scrutinizing my face, she adds, sounding amused, "Good to see that you remember your name today, Miss Miyamizu."

At that, the whole class bursts out laughing. Excuse me? Seriously, what is going on?!

"You don't remember?"

"…No."

"For real?"

"Yes, for real," I answer, taking a sip of banana juice. *Gulp.* Yum. Saya's looking at me as if I'm some inanimate oddity.

"…No, listen. Yesterday, you forgot where your desk and your locker were. Your hair was all mussed and cowlicky, and you hadn't tied it back. You didn't wear your uniform ribbon, and you were crabby the whole time."

I try visualizing what that must've looked like…… What?

"What?! No way, are you serious?!"

"Yeah, you acted like you had amnesia or somethin' yesterday."

Flustered, I try to think back… Something really is off here. I can't remember yesterday. Or, no—I do remember little bits and pieces.

There was…an unfamiliar town somewhere?

A reflection in a mirror…a boy?

I try to retrace my memories. *Piihyororooo.* In the distance, a kite mocks me. It's lunchtime, and we're chatting in a corner of the schoolyard, juice boxes in hand.

"Umm… It feels like I spent the whole day in this weird dream. Like…a dream about somebody else's life? …Mm, I can't remember much of it…"

"I got it!"

Tesshi shouts all of a sudden, and I jump. He snatches up his half-read issue of the occult magazine *MU* and shoves it under our noses, spit flying enthusiastically.

"Memories of your past life! That's what that is! Yeah, I know you're gonna say that ain't scientific, but if you put it another way and say your unconscious mind got linked up with a multiverse based on Everett's many-worlds interpretation—"

"You shut your piehole," Saya scolds him sharply.

"Hey! Were you the one who scribbled in my notebook?!" I erupt at almost the same time.

"Huh? Scribbled?"

Oh, I guess not. Tesshi's not the type to pull a lame prank like that, and he didn't have a motive, either.

"Um, nothin'. Never mind," I say, backing down.

"Say what? Whaddaya mean, 'scribbled'? Am I a suspect for somethin'?"

"I told you, forget it."

"Whoa, Mitsuha, you're so mean! Did you hear that, Saya? I've been falsely accused! Framed! Call a prosecutor, gimme a prosecutor! Or wait, maybe that's a lawyer. Hey, which one are you supposed to get for stuff like this?"

"Anyway, Mitsuha, you really were kinda funny yesterday," Saya says, grandly ignoring Tesshi's complaints. "Were you feelin' sick?"

"Hmm… That's so weird. Maybe I really am stressed…"

I think back on all the accounts I've gotten so far.

Tesshi's already absorbed in his magazine again, as if nothing ever happened. That's one of his virtues, the way he just lets stuff go.

"That's gotta be it! You've had all kinds of stress lately!"

She's right. Even setting aside the election, that ritual's tonight! Why, oh why, in this tiny little town, do I have to have a father who's the mayor and a grandmother who's the chief Shinto priestess at the shrine? I bury my face in my knees and heave a deep, deep sigh.

"Aaagh… I wanna hurry up and graduate and go to Tokyo. This town is too cramped and too tight!"

Saya's nodding along: *I know. I totally, totally get it!* "My mom and my sisters have all been in charge of the town broadcasts, one after another. Ever since I was tiny, the neighborhood ladies have called me 'the little broadcast girl,' you know?! And now I'm in the broadcastin' club for some reason! Even I don't know what I want to do anymore!"

"Saya, once we graduate, let's get out and go to Tokyo together! Even when we're grown up, in this town, we'll still be stuck with the school hierarchy! We'll never be free of these moldy old traditions! C'mon, Tesshi, you're comin' with us, right?"

"Hmm?" Absently, Tesshi looks up from his magazine.

"…Were you even listenin'?"

"Mm. I don't really, uh… I think I'll just live here for the rest of my life."

HAAAAAAAAH. Saya and I sigh again. This is why he isn't popular with girls… Although it's not like I've ever had a boyfriend myself.

The wind whispers gently. When I turn to look after it, there's Itomori Lake below us: placid, calm, and completely disinterested.

This town doesn't have a bookstore or a dentist. There's one train every two hours, buses come through only twice each day, we don't get weather reports for our area, and we're still a mosaic on the Google Maps satellite photos. The convenience store closes at nine, and it sells things like vegetable seeds and high-grade farming equipment.

On the way home from school, Saya and I are still in "griping about Itomori" mode.

There are no big chains like McDonald's or MOS Burger, but we have two sleazy "snack bars." There's no work, no girls come here to find husbands, and the daylight hours are short. Gripe, gripe, gripe, gripe. Most of the time, we actually find the town's sparse population refreshing. We're almost proud of it, but today we despair in earnest.

Tesshi's been pushing his bike along after us, off in his own world, and he irritably cuts into the conversation.

"Geez, y'all!"

"What?" we ask crossly, and Tesshi gives a creepy grin.

"Forget about all that stuff. Wanna stop at the café?"

"Huh…?"

"Wha…?"

"Wha…?!"

"A café?!" we chorus in perfect unison.

A metallic *kachonk!* melts into the calls of the evening cicadas. "Here." Tesshi holds out the cans of juice from the vending machine. With a motorized whine, an old man riding his electric scooter home from the fields crosses in front of us, and a passing stray dog sits down and yawns as if to say, *Yeah, why not? I'll keep you company.*

The "café" wasn't exactly what springs to mind. It wasn't Starbucks or Tully's or one of those fantastic, fabled spaces that serves pancakes and bagels and gelato. It was just a neighborhood bus stop out in the middle of nowhere with a vending machine and a bench with an ice-cream sign from about thirty years ago plastered to it. The three of us sit side by side on the bench, sipping our juice, while the dog rests at our feet. We don't feel like Tesshi tricked us. It's more like, *Well, sure. What else would it be?*

"Okay, I'm headin' home."

I bid my farewells to the two of them after participating in an exchange I could not have cared less about—*"I think it's about a degree cooler than it was yesterday." "No, I think it's a degree warmer"*—that lasted as long as it took to finish a can of juice.

"Good luck tonight," says Saya.

"We'll come by and watch later," promises Tesshi.

"You seriously don't have to! Actually, don't you dare!" I warn them, but inside, I'm sending a prayer in their direction. Do your best to turn into an actual couple, you two! After climbing the stone steps for a while, I turn back, looking at the pair of them as they sit on the bench with the sunset-colored lake in the background, and I softly layer a lyrical piano melody over the scene. Mm-hmm, y'all really do look good together. Tonight, I must perform my awful duty, but I hope you can enjoy your youth.

"Awww, I wanna do it, too," Yotsuha grumbles.

"It's too soon for you yet, Yotsuha," hushes Gran.

The constant click of spherical weights knocking together echoes in a workroom big enough for only about eight tatami mats. "Listen to the voice of the thread," Gran tells her. Even as she speaks, her hands don't pause in their work. "If you keep windin' threads that way, before long, emotions will start runnin' between you and the thread."

"Huh? But thread doesn't talk."

"Our braided cords—," Gran continues, ignoring Yotsuha's objection. All three of us are wearing kimonos, and we're finishing up the cords that we'll use in tonight's ceremony.

Braided cords are made of thin threads plaited together into a single rope. It's a traditional folk art that's been handed down for a very long time. The finished cords are cute and colorful, with all sorts of designs braided into them. That said, the work takes quite a bit of skill, so Gran's making Yotsuha's for her. Yotsuha's spending the time doing assistant work, winding thread around the ball-weights.

"Our braided cords hold a thousand years of Itomori's history. I tell you, that school of yours really should put priority on teachin' this sort of town history to you children. Listen, two hundred years ago…"

Here we go again, I think with a wry little smile. It's Gran's favorite speech, and I've heard it over and over in this workroom, ever since I was small.

"A fire began in the bathroom of Mayugorou Yamazaki, the straw sandal–maker, and it burned up this whole area, including the shrine and all the old records. It was what people call—"

Gran glances at me.

"'The Great Mayugorou Fire,'" I answer smoothly.

Mm-hmm. Gran nods, looking satisfied.

"What? They named the fire after him?!" Yotsuha exclaims, startled. "Poor Mr. Mayugorou," she mutters. "Havin' his name stick around 'cause of somethin' like that."

"Thanks to that fire, we don't know what our dances or the patterns in our cords mean anymore. All we have left are the forms. Still, even not knowin', we mustn't ever let the forms disappear. The meanin' in those shapes is bound to resurface someday."

Gran's words have a unique rhythm to them, like a traditional ballad, and as I braid my cord, I mouth the words along with her, silently reciting them from memory. *The meanin' in those shapes is bound to resurface someday. Here, at Miyamizu Shrine—*

"Here, at Miyamizu Shrine, that's our solemn duty. And yet…"

At that point, Gran lowers her mild eyes, sadly.

"And yet, that foolish son of mine… As if abandonin' the priesthood and leavin' this house weren't enough, he had to become a politician…"

Gran sighs, and I sneak a small sigh of my own underneath it. Even I don't really know whether I love this town or hate it, whether I want to go somewhere far away or stay with my family and friends forever. When I remove my finished, brightly colored cord from the round stand, it makes a soft, lonely *click*.

I think the sound of the wooden Japanese flute that drifts from the shrine in the darkness would probably terrify city folks. It sets the mood for some sinister event, like in an old murder mystery novel. For a little while now, I've been performing a ceremonial shrine

maiden dance, feeling gloomy enough that I wish a killer like Jason
or Jack the Ripper—anybody really—would just put me out of my
misery.

This time every year, the Miyamizu Shrine holds its harvest festival, and Yotsuha and I have the misfortune of being the stars of
the show. On this day, we wear crisp shrine maiden outfits, paint on
bright-red lip rouge and wear jingly hair ornaments, go out in front
of the standing audience at the *kagura* hall, and dance the dance
Gran taught us. It's one of the traditions whose meaning was lost
in the fire, and it's performed by two people, moving in sync. We're
both holding bells with colorful cords tied to them. We ring them,
twirling around and around, making the cords flare out and trail
behind us. During my last spin, I spotted Tesshi and Saya out of the
corner of my eye and got even more depressed. Those little— I told
them and told them not to come, and they're still here?! I'll hex them
with my shrine maiden power! I'll text them tons of curse stamps
with Line! That said, the dance isn't the part I hate. Sure, it's a little
embarrassing, but since I've been doing it since I was little, I'm completely used to it. No, it's not this. It's that one ritual. The one that's
more embarrassing the older I get. That thing I have to do right after
this. The part that seems intentionally designed to brutally humiliate
women.

Oh, for the love of—

I don't wanna!

Plagued by these thoughts, I move my body, and then all of a
sudden, the dance ends. Agh. Here it comes.

Munch, munch, munch.
Munch.
Munch, munch, munch, munch.

I'm intently chewing rice. I shut my eyes and keep chewing, trying not to think, trying not to sense flavor or sound or color. Beside
me, Yotsuha's doing the exact same thing. We're kneeling formally,

side by side, and a small wooden box rests on a stand in front of each of us. And of course, beyond that, a diverse audience of all ages and genders stares at us.

Munch, munch, munch.

Munch, munch.

Agh, I swear…

Munch, munch, munch.

I'm going to have to do it soon.

Munch, munch.

Arrrgh.

Munch.

Giving up, I raise the box in front of me. I bring it close to my lips, attempting to veil my mouth with the sleeve of my kimono.

And then. Aaagh.

Puckering my lips, I spit the rice I've been chewing into the box. The mixture of grain and saliva dribbles from my mouth as a thick, white liquid. I feel as if I've heard the crowd stir, muttering. *Waaaaaaaaah!* I sob internally. Please, nobody look at me.

Mouth-brewed sake.

It's the oldest type of sake in Japan. If you chew up rice, mixing it with saliva, then just let it sit, it ferments and turns into alcohol. Then it's offered to the gods. Long ago, I hear places all over the country used to make it, but I don't know if any other shrines still do this sort of thing now, in the twenty-first century… And seriously, doing it in shrine maiden clothes is just over the top! I mean, what's the point?! Mentally sniffling, I pick up another pinch of rice and put it in my mouth like a trooper. Then I chew again. Yotsuha is doing the exact same thing, her expression cool and composed. We have to do this over and over until the tiny boxes are full. *Dribble…* I spit saliva and rice again. Inside, I'm crying my eyes out.

Abruptly, my ears catch familiar voices. Feeling a bad premonition like a faint ripple, I raise my eyes ever so slightly.

Curses.

I want to explode and take the shrine with me. I knew it: It's my three flashy "in-crowd" classmates. They're watching me with smirks on their faces and gleefully gossiping about something. There's too much distance between us for me to really hear them but I feel as though I'm hearing them loud and clear. *Eeeeee, I could never, ever do that!* and *That's kinda obscene,* and *Man, how can she do that in public? Nobody's ever gonna marry her now.*

I make a very, very firm resolution:

When I graduate, I am leaving this town and going far away.

"Cheer up, Sis. Who cares if people from your school saw you? And anyway, what's got you so shook up?"

"It must be nice being a carefree, prepubescent little kid!"

I glare at Yotsuha. We've changed into T-shirts and just left the shrine office entrance.

After the harvest festival, to close out the night, the two of us attended a banquet for the local men and women who helped with the festival. Gran was the hostess, and Yotsuha and I poured sake and made conversation.

"How old are you now, li'l Mitsuha? What?! Seventeen?! I see… Havin' a sweet young thing like you pour for me makes me feel young again."

"Yessir, go on and roll the years way back! Here, go ahead—drink some more!"

We entertained almost desperately, wore ourselves out, and they finally turned us loose just now, saying, "You kids can go on home." Gran and the other adults are still at the shrine office, carrying on with the banquet.

"Yotsuha, do you know what the average age was back there, in the office?"

On the grounds, all the lights on the shrine approach are out, and the cool sounds of insect songs echo all around us.

"I dunno. Sixty?"

"I did the math in the kitchen. It was seventy-eight. Seventy-eight!"

"Huh."

"Now that we're gone, it's ninety-one in there! They're pushin' a hundred. They're in the final stage of life. The underworld might send a reaper for the whole place!"

"Hmm…"

What I'm trying to get at is that we should bail on this town ASAP, but Yotsuha's response is terse. She seems preoccupied with something else. Well, she's just a little kid. She wouldn't understand her big sister's agony. Giving up, I look at the sky. The vast expanse of it is filled with dazzling bright stars, shining transcendentally, as if human lives on Earth are none of their concern.

"…That's it!"

As we descend the shrine's long stone stairway, side by side, Yotsuha suddenly cries out. She's wearing a triumphant expression, as if having found a cake someone hid from her.

"Sis, why don't you chew up a whole bunch of that sake and use it to pay your way to Tokyo?!"

For a moment, I'm speechless.

"…You've got quite the mind to come up with that."

"You could send snapshots and 'makin' of' documentary videos with it and call it 'Shrine Maiden Sake' or somethin'! I bet that'd sell!"

Should I be worried that my nine-year-old sister sees the world like that? Still, I realize Yotsuha is actually concerned about me, in her own way. *Aw, she really is cute*, I think, a little more fondly than before. Okay then, maybe I'll give this sake business idea some serious thought… Wait, can you just sell sake on your own like that?

"Well? What do you think, Sis?"

"Hmm…"

…And that's all I have to say.

"…Wait, no! It'd be against the liquor laws!"

Wait, was that the problem? I wonder, and when I come back to myself, I've broken into a run. All sorts of incidents and feelings and prospects and doubts and despairs are jumbled together inside me, and it feels like my heart's about to explode. I run down the steps, taking them two at a time, slam on the brakes under the *torii* gate on the landing, and suck in a huge lungful of chilly night air. Then I expel the cluttered mess in my chest along with it.

"I'm sick of this town! I'm sick of this life! Make me a hot guy in Tokyo in my next life, puhleeeease!"

Eeease. Eeease. Eeease. Eeease...

My wish echoes around the dark mountains, then disappears as though drawn into Itomori Lake below me. The words came out on impulse, and they're so dumb, my head cools right down, as does my sweat.

Oh, but even so.

Gods, if you're really there…

Please—

Even if the gods really do exist, I still don't know what to wish for.

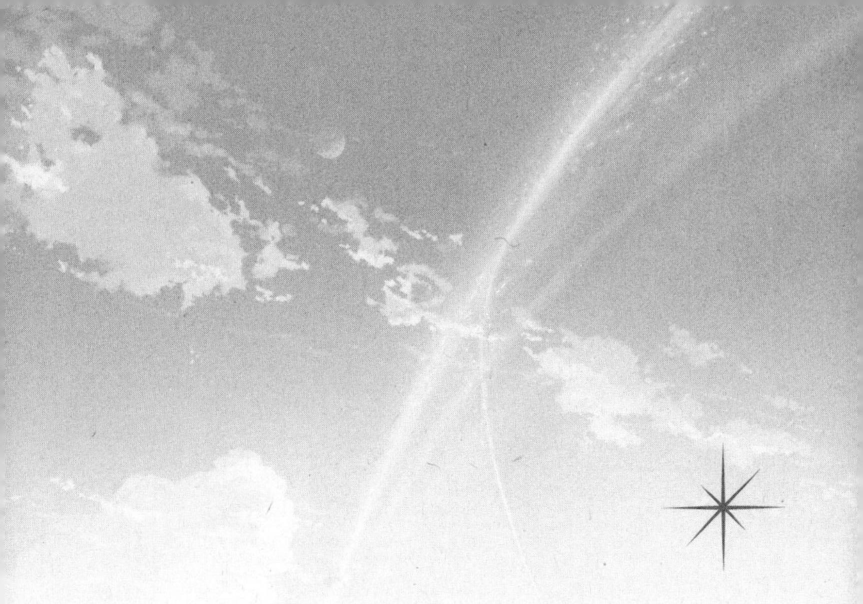

Chapter Three

Days

I don't recognize that ringtone, I think drowsily.

An alarm? But I'm still sleepy. And you know what, I'm going right back to sleep. Eyes still shut, I grope for the smartphone I know I put beside my futon.

Huh?

I reach farther. Grr, that alarm is so noisy. Where'd I put it?

"—Ow!"

My back hits the floor with an emphatic *thud*. Apparently, I've managed to fall out of bed. Ow, ow, ow, ow... Wait, what? Bed?

I finally open my eyes and sit up.

Huh?

The room is completely unfamiliar.

And I'm in it.

Did I sleep over somewhere last night?

"...Where am I?"

The moment I murmur the words, I notice a strange heaviness in my throat. By reflex, I put a hand to it. The throat my fingers find is hard and angular. "Hmm?" My voice slips out again, and it's really low. I look down at myself.

...They're gone.

A T-shirt I've never seen before falls flat all the way to my stomach, and they're not there.

My boobs are gone.

And right in the middle of my freakishly visible lower body, there's…something. Something asserting its presence strongly enough to overwrite the feeling of wrongness precipitated by my missing boobs.

What is…this?

Slowly, I extend my hand, reaching for that area. All the blood in my body and all the skin over it is being pulled toward that one spot.

…Is this, um…? L-location-wise, it's…

. . . .

. . . .

. . . . . .

I touch it.

And very nearly pass out.

Who is this guy?

I'm gazing at a strange face in the mirror of a strange bathroom.

His slightly showy hairstyle brushes his eyebrows, apparently aiming for a casual/calculated ratio of about 6:4. The eyebrows are stubborn-looking, but his eyes are on the wide side and make him seem like a bit of a pushover. His chapped lips seem completely unacquainted with the concept of moisturizer, and his neck looks stiff. His cheeks are lean, with clean lines, and for some reason, there's a big bandage on one of them. When I touch it gingerly, there's a dull throb.

—But. Even though it hurts, I don't wake up. My throat is bone-dry. I twist the faucet, fill my hands with tap water, and drink. It's unpleasantly warm and smells like chemicals, like pool water.

"Taki, are you up?"

Abruptly, a man's voice calls from somewhere in the distance, and I give a little shriek of alarm. Taki?

"Breakfast was your job today, kid. Remember? You overslept."

Nervously, I peek into what looks like a living room. As he speaks, a middle-aged man in a suit glances at me, then immediately returns his attention to the dishes.

"I-I'm sorry!"

I apologize out of habit.

"I'm heading out. There's miso soup—go ahead and finish it off."

"Um, yessir."

"And go to school. Even if you're late."

On that note, the man briskly piles up the dishes, puts them in the small kitchen, passes by me as I stand petrified in the doorway, goes to the foyer, dons his shoes, opens the door, steps out, and shuts it behind him. It all happens so fast there'd have been barely enough time for a kite to call once.

"…What a weird dream," I say out loud.

I take another look around the room. There are photos and design sketches of bridges and buildings and structures all over the walls. The floor is a careless mess of magazines and paper bags and cardboard boxes. Compared to the Miyamizu house, tidy as a venerable old Japanese inn (all thanks to Gran), this place seems wild and lawless. The room is really small—probably a condominium. If this is my dream, I have no idea where it came from, but I'm impressed by how real it seems. I guess I've got a pretty good imagination. Maybe I could be some kind of artist when I grow up.

Tweedle!

A text alert echoes from the depths of the hall with such impeccable timing that it seems like a comeback. *Eep!* I gasp, hastily dashing back to the room where the bed was. The smartphone's on the floor beside the sheets, and there's a short message on its screen.

Are you still home? Get over here, run! Tsukasa

Huh? What? What's this? Who in the world is Tsukasa?!

At any rate, I guess I have to go to school. I scan the room. My eyes stop on a boy's uniform hanging beside the window, and as I pick it up, I'm suddenly aware of another emergency.

Oh, for the love of…!

I need to pee.

Haaaaaah. I heave a sigh nearly strong enough to deflate my whole body.

What is *wrong* with guys' bodies, anyway?!

I managed to do my business somehow, but I'm still shaking with anger. The harder I tried to pee, and the more I tried to aim it with my fingers, the more the thing changed shape and the harder it got to go. What's up with that?! Are they stupid?! Are they idiots?! Or is this guy weird?! Arrrgh! I'd never even seen one of those before! And excuse me, but I'm technically a shrine maiden!

After I change into the uniform, keeping my head bent from the awful shame and fighting back tears (I can't actually fight them all back, and a few slip out), I open the condo's door. *Well, for now, I'll just go*, I think, and raise my head.

—And then.

My eyes are riveted.

The view before me leaves me breathless.

I'm standing on the outside corridor of a high-rise condo that's probably on a hill.

Below lies a generous carpet of greenery, like a large park. The sky is a vivid cerulean blue, without the slightest blemish. On the border between the blue and green, ranks of buildings of all sizes line up neatly, like extra-intricate origami. Each and every one is stamped with minute, exquisite windows like the mesh of a net. Some of the windows reflect blue, others are tinted green, and still others simply glitter in the morning sun. I can see a red tower, tiny with distance, and a silver building whose rounded lines remind me vaguely of a whale, and a shining black building that looks as though it's been cut from a block of obsidian. I'm sure these buildings and several of the others are famous—even I recognize some of them. Far away, little toy cars flow in neat, orderly lines.

It's the scenery of the biggest city in Japan, and compared with what I'd imagined, it's— Actually, come to think of it, I've never really tried to visualize what it would be like before, but it's much, much more beautiful than it looks in the movies and on TV. It hits me hard, right in the chest.

"Tokyo," I murmur.

This world is far too dazzling. I inhale deeply and squint, as if looking at the sun.

"Hey, where'd you buy this?" "In Nishi-Azabu, on the way home from lessons." "Guess who's gonna be opening for their next big concert?" "Yo, wanna skip club today and go catch a movie?" "An agency employee is coming to the mixer tonight."

Wh-what's with these conversations? Are these people actually modern Japanese high schoolers? Maybe they're just reading posts off some celebrity's Facebook page?

I watch the classroom from where I'm standing, half-hidden behind the door, timing my entrance. I used my smartphone's GPS to get here, and even then, I got incredibly lost. By the time I found the school, the lunch bell was already chiming away.

Still, this school— Glass windows that take up entire walls, bare concrete, colorful iron doors with round windows... It's so abnormally fancy, I have to wonder whether it's a World Expo venue or something. This Taki Tachibana guy, a boy my age, lives in a world like this? I think of his name, which I found in his student handbook, and his smug expression on his ID photo. They annoy me a little.

"Taaaki!"

"——!"

Somebody abruptly throws an arm around my shoulders from behind, and I give a wordless yelp. When I look, a bespectacled CEO-type (only neat and sophisticated) is smiling at me, close enough that our bangs are almost touching. Eeeeeek! 'Scuse me, mister—this is the closest I've ever been to a guy in my life!

"Look at you, showing up at noon. Let's go eat."

With that, the kid with glasses sets off down the hall, still hugging my shoulders. No, seriously, you're way too close!

"Ignore my text, will you?" he accuses, but he doesn't sound mad. Then I figure it out.

"…Excuse me… Wait, Tsukasa?"

"Ha-ha, 'excuse me'? Do I detect a note of contrition?"

I don't know how to respond to that, so for the moment, I quietly extricate myself from his arm.

"…You got lost?"

Takagi—a big, good-natured guy—shouts, not bothering to hide his astonishment.

"How the heck did you manage to get lost on the way to school?"

"Um…" I falter. The three of us are sitting in a corner of the wide rooftop. It's supposed to be lunchtime right now, but there aren't many people around. Maybe they're avoiding the summer sun.

"Oh, um, 'scuse me—"

"'Scuse me'?"

Takagi and Tsukasa eye each other dubiously. Oops, that's right: I'm Taki Tachibana now.

"Uh, I mean, um… Oh. Pardon me…?"

"Hunh?"

"Sorry……"

"Say what?"

"……Whatever?"

Uh-huh, they nod, still looking bewildered. I see, so he's the "whatever" type. Got it!

"I was just enjoyin' myself a little. Tokyo's kinda like a festival. Real lively."

"…What's with the accent?" asks Takagi.

"Huh?!" I have an accent? I turn red.

"Taki, where's your lunch?" Tsukasa prods.

"Huh?!!" I didn't bring one!

As I hunt through my school bag, sweating bullets, they laugh. "Do you have a fever or something?"

"Tsukasa, you got anything?"

"Egg sandwich. Let's stick that croquette of yours in here."

Here. The two of them hand me the improvised egg-croquette sandwich. Their kindness touches my heart.

"Thank you…"

They both grin at me wordlessly. To think boys could be so stylish and kind…! No, Mitsuha, don't do it! Don't fall for both of them at once! —Well, no, I'm not falling for anybody, but Tokyo is fantastic, anyway!

"So listen, after class today, wanna go to that café again?" Takagi asks, and without thinking, I stare at him as he takes a bite of rice.

"Yeah, good idea," Tsukasa replies. Taking a swig of water out of a plastic bottle, his throat works smoothly. Huh? What? Where did he say we were going?

"What about you, Taki? You're coming, right?"

"Huh?!"

"To the café."

"C-c-caféeeee?!"

The furrows between their eyebrows deepen, but I ignore it. My mood is soaring, and I can't repress my excitement. This is it! Who's laughing now, bus stop café?!

Two tiny dogs dressed in pop idol–style outfits are sitting on a wicker chair, watching me with eyes like candy drops and wagging their tails so hard they seem liable to come off. There's an incredible amount of space between each table, and fully half the customers are foreign. A third are wearing sunglasses, three-fifths are wearing hats, and not one is wearing a suit. There's no telling what any of them do for a living.

What is this place? Adults go to cafés with their little dogs on weekdays, in broad daylight?!

"I like the timberwork on the ceiling."

"Yeah. They put serious effort into that."

Tsukasa and Takagi don't seem the least bit intimidated by this supremely trendy space. They're smiling and discussing their impressions of the interior. Apparently, these boys are touring different cafés because they're interested in architecture. What kind of hobby is that?! Aren't high school guys into magazines like *MU*?!

"Taki, do you know what you want?"

Prompted by Tsukasa, I stop dissecting the café and let my eyes fall to the heavy, leather-bound menu.

"…! I—I could live for a month on how much these pancakes cost!"

"What era are you from, again?" Takagi laughs.

"Umm…"

I stress about it for a little while and then remember: *Oh. Right. This is a dream.* Well, in that case, why not? It's Taki Tachibana's money anyway. I'll just eat whatever I want.

Ahhhh, what a great dream…

The pancakes are the heavyweight kind, a fortress solidly flanked by things like mango and blueberries. After finishing them, I sip cinnamon coffee, deeply satisfied.

Tweedle.

The smartphone in my pocket chirps... Huh. There are an awful lot of angry-vein symbols in this text.

"...Agh! What'll I do? It says I'm late for work! Somebody who's probably my boss is mad at me!"

"Wait, you had a shift today?" asks Takagi.

"You better hurry and go, then," says Tsukasa.

"Right!" I hastily stand. Oh, but...

"What's up?"

"Umm... Where do I work again?"

".......Say what?"

The two boys have soared past disgust. They seem about ready to snap. Gimme a break. I know absolutely nothing about this guy!

"Excuse me—isn't our order ready yet?"

"Taki! Go take table twelve's order!"

"This isn't what I asked for."

"Taki! I told you, we're out of the truffles!"

"Is our check ready yet?"

"Taki, you're in the way! Move!"

"Taki, you idiot, do your job!"

"Taki!"

The place is a dauntingly ritzy Italian restaurant.

It's a two-story building that's open all the way up, atrium-style. The ceiling is hung with sparkling chandeliers, and there are big propellers up there, too, spinning slowly. I've seen something like them in a movie. Taki Tachibana is a bow tie–wearing waiter, and at dinnertime, the restaurant is hellishly busy.

I'm being swept this way and that by a muddy torrent of confusion, getting orders wrong, serving them wrong, getting *tsk*ed at by customers and yelled at by the chefs. Come on, people, I've never worked here before! Actually, I've never worked a part-time job before, period! This is a total nightmare! Waaaah, seriously, when am I gonna wake up?! This is all your fault, stupid Taki Tachibana!

"—'Scuse me. You. Boy."

"Huh? Uh, yes?!"

I've already gone a little ways past the customer who flagged me down, and I turn back hastily. How am I supposed to know to respond to "boy," huh?

Wow. The man's an obvious thug, complete with open-collared shirt, gold chain, and lots of clunky rings. Still, if you go to the next city over from my town, there are a lot of guys like him hanging out in front of the station. His type feels a little more familiar to me than the celebrity-esque luster of the other customers. When he speaks, there's a thin smarm in his voice:

"Listen. There was a toothpick in my pizza."

"Huh?"

Mr. Thug picks up the very last slice of basil pizza with his fingertips. There's a toothpick sticking out of the edge where it was sliced, basically screaming that someone jabbed it in there after the fact. Maybe he's joking around with me. I'm bewildered, unsure how to respond, and Mr. Thug continues with a seemingly fixed smile.

"It woulda been bad if I'd eaten that, right? We're just lucky I noticed it. What're you gonna do?"

"Huh…?"

I get the feeling I really can't afford to say, *You really stuck that in there yourself, right, sir?* I give a noncommittal smile instead… Conversely, his fades.

"I'm asking you what you're gonna do about it?!"

Crash! All of a sudden, he kicks the table up with his knee and starts yelling. Instantly, the murmur of conversation freezes. I tense up, too.

"—Sir! Is something the matter?"

A woman appears and pushes me out of the way. She glances at me and whispers, "I've got this!"

Someone else grabs my arm from behind and drags me away—a waiter who's probably worked there longer than me. "You're acting pretty weird today," he says, looking concerned.

"I'm terribly sorry about that, sir!" Out of the corner of my eye, I see the woman bowing deeply to the thug.

The background hum returns, as if someone's twisted the volume back up.

I'm pushing an industrial vacuum cleaner that's as big as a lawn mower over the floor. The restaurant's finally closed. The lights in the chandeliers have dimmed, and all the tables have been stripped. One employee polishes glasses, another checks the stock in the refrigerator, and somebody else is doing something with the computers at the cashier counter.

The woman who rescued me is wiping down the tables one by one. For a little while now, I've been trying—and failing—to find an opportunity to speak to her. Her long hair has a soft wave to it. From the side, it hides her eyes, and I can't read her expression. Still, her lustrous, glossy lips are curved into a gentle smile. Her arms and legs are slender, and her waist is very small—and yet she's got big boobs. She's just incredibly cool somehow. Passing her, I catch a glimpse of the name tag on that proud bosom. It reads *Okudera*. Perfect!

"Miss Okudera?"

Just as I take the plunge and speak, somebody pokes me in the back of the head.

"That's *senpai* to you!" The guy who poked me sounds like he's joking. He goes back into the kitchen, a stack of menus in one hand. I see, so she's got seniority on me. Okay!

"Um, Okudera-senpai! That was really…"

"Taki. You had a rough day today, didn't you?"

As she speaks, she turns and looks me right in the eye. Her long eyelashes curve toward the ceiling, her perfectly shaped almond eyes are the epitome of beauty, and her sexy voice sends a tickle down my back. I instinctively feel compelled to tell her *I love you!* My cheeks flush a little, and I hastily look down.

"Uh, no, it wasn't really 'rough,' just…"

"That guy was totally full of it. I handled it according to the manual and let him have his food for free, but…"

She doesn't seem all that angry. She flips the rag over and starts wiping down another table. Just as I'm about to try to prolong the conversation…

"Eek! Okudera-senpai!"

Another waitress cries out.

"Your skirt!"

"Hmm?"

Miss Okudera twists to inspect her rear, and her face rapidly flushes. Now that I'm looking, I can see a rough, horizontal slash just above her thigh. With a shocked little shriek, she pulls her apron around to hide the tear.

"Are you hurt?"

"Geez! Nasty. Was it that one dude?"

"I think something like that's happened before…"

"Was someone harassing you?"

"Do you remember the guy's face?"

Several staff members gather around Okudera-senpai, chattering worriedly. Eyes downcast, she's gone very still. I stand motionless, like an idiot, with the words I'd prepared still on my tongue. Her shoulders tremble slightly. I think I see little tears welling up at the corners of her eyes.

This time, I need to rescue her.

The thought seems to burst inside me, and before I know what I'm doing, I've grabbed Okudera-senpai's hand and started walking. I hear voices at my back ("Hey! Taki, you little…"), but I ignore them.

*   *   *

The green can be a field. The orange is flowers and butterflies. I want at least one more design element. The brown is— Sure, it'll be a hedgehog. The cream is for its nose.

Pinching the edges of the tear in the skirt, I deftly whipstitch it together. For some reason, there were several colors of embroidery thread in the changing room sewing kit, so I'm taking the opportunity to make this a bit of an elaborate repair job. Gran trained me in needlework, and it's something I'm particularly good at.

"All done!"

I hand the skirt to Miss Okudera. It's only taken me about five minutes to finish.

"...Huh? This is..."

The dubious expression she's worn since I dragged her to the dressing room quickly shifts to surprise.

"This is amazing! Taki, wow! It's even cuter than it was before!"

The tear in the skirt was a straight, horizontal line about six inches long, so as I stitched it together, I turned it into a scene of a hedgehog playing in a field. The skirt is dark brown, so the little decoration acts as an accent, my thought being a cute motif would look especially good on a sophisticated beauty like Okudera-senpai. She has an even-featured, gorgeous, magazine-model face, but when she smiles, she's more approachable, like an older girl from the neighborhood.

"You really saved me today. Thank you very much."

I finally managed to say it.

"Heh-heh!" Okudera-senpai's large eyes narrow softly when she smiles. "To tell you the truth, I was a little worried back there. You're weak, Taki, but you're always so quick to fight."

As she speaks, her slim fingers lightly tap her left cheek. Oh. Vaguely, I grasp the reason for the bandage on Taki Tachibana's face.

"I like this version of you better," Okudera-senpai says, a bit mischievously. "You're surprisingly in touch with your feminine side, Taki."

My heart leaps with a *bo-yo-yoing*. Her smile is absolutely unbeatable. It makes me want to give her everything I have for free. I think it's the most precious thing I've seen in Tokyo today.

The yellow train I take to get home is empty.

By now, I've realized that Tokyo is filled with all sorts of scents. Convenience stores, family restaurants, the people I pass, the edge of the park, construction sites, the station at night, the inside of the train... Almost every ten steps, the aromas change. I never knew human beings had such pronounced smells when gathered in one place.

And for every lighted window that skims past my vision, there's a person living in this city. My heart is strangely stirred by the ranks of buildings that stretch as far as the eye can see, by their dizzying numbers and the overwhelming weight of them, almost like a mountain range.

Taki Tachibana is one of the residents here, too. Softly, I extend a hand toward the boy reflected in the train window. His face annoyed me a little, but I guess I don't hate it. I'm starting to feel a sense of camaraderie with this guy, as if he's a fellow soldier who endured this rough day with me. But you know—

"Y'know, this is a really impressive dream, if I do say so myself."

Back at his house, I throw myself onto the bed where I woke up this morning.

I'll tell Tesshi and Saya about all this tomorrow: *Listen to this dream I had! Isn't that amazin'? Aren't you awed by my fantastic imagination?! It's like I actually went to Tokyo! I bet I'm gonna be a manga artist—or no, wait, I'm not so great at art, but I bet writin' novels would be a cakewalk. I'll probably make a ton of money! You wanna be my roommates in Tokyo?*

Fantasizing about this and grinning to myself, I roll over onto my back, pick up Taki Tachibana's smartphone, and start skimming through it with my fingertip. Oh look, he keeps a diary.

[9/7 Ate at KFC with Tsukasa and Co.] [9/6 Movie in Hibiya] [8/31 Architecture Tour—Bayside Edition] [8/25 Payday!]

As I scroll backward through the headers, I'm impressed in spite of myself. "He's real thorough." Then I tap the photo app. Most of the pictures are landscapes. After those, the majority are of him with Tsukasa and Takagi. Eating ramen together, going to the park together… They sure are close. A beef bowl place, a soba shop at the station, a trendy hamburger joint. The road home from school. Sunset through the gaps between the buildings. His friends' backs. Jet contrails in the sky overhead.

"Lucky him, livin' in Tokyo…"

As I murmur, a yawn slips out. Starting to get sleepy, I go to the next photo.

"Oh, it's Okudera-senpai."

The picture is of her back as she's cleaning the restaurant window, and it feels like a candid shot. In the next, she's noticed and turned to face the camera, beaming and flashing a peace sign.

…*Maybe he likes Okudera-senpai*, I think out of nowhere. It's bound to be unrequited, though. She's in college. To her, high school guys are still just kids.

I sit up on the bed and create an entry in his diary app. Then I start typing in everything I experienced today. About how I made a lot of mistakes but connected with Okudera-senpai at the end. About how, on the way home from work, we walked from the restaurant to the station together. I capture all of it in the entry, wanting to report it—or brag about it—to Taki Tachibana. Once I'm done, I yawn again. Then, out of nowhere…

*   *   *

Who are you?

For some reason, I remember the line scribbled in my Japanese notebook. Vaguely, I can picture Taki Tachibana in my body, writing that note in my room in Itomori before he falls asleep. What a bizarre idea. Still, there's something oddly persuasive about it. I take a felt-tip marker from the desk, and on the palm of my hand, I write:

Mitsuha

Yaaaawwn...

That's the third yawn. Unsurprisingly, today wore me out. It was a colorful, thrilling day. It feels as if I spent all of it getting pelted by a rainbow-colored shower. Even without background music, this world dazzled me from start to finish. I imagine how startled Taki Tachibana's going to react when he sees the writing on his hand, and, smiling a little, I fall asleep.

✳   ✳   ✳

"...What is this?"

I say the words aloud, despite myself. I'm staring at my hand.

Finally, I let my eyes drop from the letters on my palm down to my wrinkled uniform and necktie... So, what—I fell asleep without changing?

"—Wh...wh-what is this?!"

This time, I actually yell. We're having breakfast, and my dad glances at me but promptly loses interest and returns his attention to his bowl. I stare at my phone, stunned. There's a really long journal entry on it that I don't remember writing.

...And on the way home from work, Okudera-senpai and I walked to the station together, just the two of us! It's all because I'm in touch with my feminine side. ♡

"Taki, want to hit another café today?"

"Uh, sorry, I've got work after this."

"Ha-ha. You know where to go?"

"Huh? ...Hey! Tsukasa, you jerk, was that you?"

I raise my voice without meaning to. Actually, I wish it was him. Tsukasa's puzzled expression tells me it wasn't, though. Even I know there's no reason somebody'd go to all that trouble for a prank.

Getting up from my chair, I reluctantly excuse myself:

"...Nah, never mind. See ya."

As I leave the classroom, I hear Takagi's voice behind me. *Dude's back to normal today.*

An uneasy shiver shoots through me, and my feet get cold. Something very weird is happening to me.

"...Wh-what?"

After I change into my work clothes, three of my senior coworkers are standing outside the changing room when I open the door, blocking my way. There's one regular staffer and two college part-timers, all guys, and they're glaring at me with eyes that look bloodshot or maybe teary... Either way, not good. I swallow hard, and the three of them start in on me in menacing tones.

"Taki, you scumbag, whaddaya think you're doing, getting a jump on us?" "You'd better have an excuse, weasel." "You two left together yesterday, didn't you?"

"Huh... Wait, no way—seriously?! I did? With Okudera-senpai?!"

Meaning that journal entry was real?!

"What happened with you two after that?!"

"Uh, no, I...I really don't remember much..."

"Don't gimme that crap!"

Just as it looks like somebody's gonna haul me up by my shirt-front, a cool voice echoes through the hall.

"Okudera, reporting for duty."

Okudera-senpai arrives, her long, bare legs and the shoulders peeking out of her top gleaming in the light. She greets us with a smile, strappy sandals clicking pleasantly.

"Hello, everyone."

"Hi!"

She's sort of an idol at this place, and confronted with her stunning presence, the four of us reply in unison. For a moment, we almost forget about our problem. Then Okudera-senpai turns back and looks right at me.

"Let's make it another good day. Okay, Taki?"

I can almost hear a heart symbol punctuating that sentence, so sweetly delivered, followed by a wink sent my way before she disappears through the door. I turn so red, it's like somebody dumped boiling water over my head. This is way too much. I want to go polish all the glasses in the restaurant until they shine, right this minute.

"......Hey. Taki."

The guys' voices are so dark it's as though they're resounding from the depths of the Earth, and I come back to myself with a jolt.

—Not good. As the senior staff cross-examines me, almost wailing, I wonder:

What's going on here? Are they pranking me? Is everybody in on it? ...Nah, couldn't be. What'd I do while I was out of it?

What the heck is "Mitsuha"?

The birds are energetically twittering away again this morning. There's a newborn clarity to the early sun that streams in through the paper sliding doors, and the morning is peaceful, as usual. Even so, although

I've just woken up, unfamiliar writing with a quality of pure, concentrated irritation is scrawled across my arm.

Mitsuha??? What are you? Who are you????

The letters are big and messy, written roughly with a super-thick Magic Marker, from my palm all the way up to my elbow.

"Sis, what is that?"

When I look up, Yotsuha's standing in the open sliding door. I make a face that says, *That's what I want to know.*

My little sister's face replies, *Well, it doesn't really matter.*

"You're not feelin' up your boobs today, huh? Break! Fast! Time! Hurry up!"

She shuts the sliding door with a sharp *clack*, just like always, and I watch her from my futon. Huh? Boobs? I'm "not feeling them up today"? ...Excuse me? My mind produces a gratuitous image of myself happily squeezing my own boobs... B-but that's so perverted and gross!

"Mornin'!" I say as I enter the classroom.

The minute I do, all my classmates' eyes are on me. *Eep!* I give a little gasp. Wh-what? Trying to make myself small and inconspicuous, I cross to my seat by the window. I hear whispers.

"Miyamizu was really cool yesterday, huh."

"Uh-huh. I didn't think she had it in her."

"Her personality's kinda changed, though, yeah?"

"U-um, people are lookin' at me..."

"Well, what did you expect? After what you pulled yesterday, they can't help it," says Saya.

"'What I pulled yesterday'?" I ask, sitting down.

Saya peers into my face, looking puzzled and worried.

—You know...durin' art yesterday, when we were sketchin' that still life.

Huh? You really don't remember? Again? Honestly, Mitsuha, are you okay? You and me were in the same group. We were supposed to be drawin' the vase and the apples—y'know, the subject that doesn't make any sense. Except you sketched a landscape instead. Well, that bit doesn't matter. Anyway, Matsumoto's group was behind us, and they were talkin' nasty, the way they always do.

What, you want to know? Um, well, about the mayoral election.

Huh? Details? Oh, you know, how the town administration is all just figurin' out how to hand out subsidies, and it's the same no matter who does it, but how there are "some kids" whose livelihood depends on it, et cetera. Dumb stuff like that. When you heard them, you said, "That's me they're talkin' about, right?" So I said I thought it probably was. I mean, if you ask me, I'm gonna answer, right? Then, Mitsuha, what do you suppose you did?

You seriously don't remember? You kicked the desk with the vase on it right toward Matsumoto's group! And with a great big grin on your face! Matsumoto and the others got scared, and of course, the vase broke, and the whole class went dead quiet. Actually, you gave me the chills, too!

"Wh-wh-what in the world?"

I turn pale. After school, I run straight home. Yotsuha and Gran are in the living room, drinking tea without a care in the world. Glancing at them out of the corner of my eye, I run up the stairs, shut myself in my room, and open my classics notebook. *Who are you?* it still reads. I turn a few more pages.

My skin crawls. Now there's a whole two pages filled with small letters in the same handwriting. First, in big letters, *Mitsuha Miyamizu.* Then there are lots of question marks around it and bits of personal information about me.

> *Year 2, Class 3 / Teshigawara ♂, friend, occult geek, dumb but a good guy / Sayaka ♀, friend, quiet, kinda cute*

Lives with her grandma and her little sister
Yotsuha / Way out in the sticks / Her dad is
mayor / She's a shrine maiden? / Sounds like
her mom is dead / Her dad doesn't live with
them / Doesn't have many friends / Has boobs

Then, in larger letters, What the heck is this life??

I stare at the notebook. I'm trembling. The scenery of Tokyo shimmers in my mind, as faint as a rising haze. Cafés, a part-time job, guy friends, walking home with someone…

A corner of my heart catches the tail of an impossible conclusion.
"Is this…? Could we be…?"

"Is this seriously…?"

I'm holed up in my room, staring at my phone in denial. For a while now, my fingers have been shaking as if they partly belong to somebody else as I scroll through the entries in my journal app. Sandwiched between the ones I wrote, there are several headers I don't remember.

First ♡ Harajuku-Omotesando panini-rama! / At Odaiba aquarium with two boys ♡ / Observation platform tour and flea market ♡ / Visited father's workplace ♡ Kasumigaseki District!

A corner of my mind catches the tail of an inconceivable conclusion.

Could this be…?

In my dreams, are this girl and I—
In my dreams, are this boy and I—

—switching bodies?!

＊　＊　＊

The sun rises from the edge of the mountains. Little by little, the daylight washes over the lake town. The birds in the morning, the hush at midday, the insect songs in the evening, the glitter of the night sky.

The sun rises between the buildings. Little by little, the daylight glints off countless windows. The throngs of people in the morning, the hum of midday, the scents of everyday life at half-light, the sparkle of the streets at night.

Over and over, we're captivated by moments like these.

And, gradually, we learn.

Taki Tachibana—Taki—is a high school kid my age who lives in Tokyo, and…

At irregular intervals, unexpectedly, two or three times a week, I swap bodies with Mitsuha Miyamizu, who lives way out in the sticks. It triggers when we fall asleep. We have no idea what causes it.

Our memories of the time we spend switched fade as soon as we wake up. It feels like a lucid dream.

Even so, we're definitely swapping. The reactions of the people around us prove it more than anything.

Now that we're aware that we are actually switching with each other, we're starting to hold on to bits of memories from the dreams. For example, at this point, even when I'm awake, I know there's a boy named Taki who lives in Tokyo.

Now I'm positive there's a girl named Mitsuha living in a country town somewhere. I don't have any solid evidence or rational explanation, but I have this strange sense that tells me it's real.

We've also started communicating with each other. On the days when we switch, we leave diary entries or notes on each other's smartphones.

We've tried texting and calling, too, but for some reason,

neither of us could get through. Anyway, we're lucky we figured out a way to communicate at all. We both need to keep each other's lives intact and undisturbed... So we set rules.

⟨To Taki—Don'ts List #1⟩
- Absolutely no baths, ever.
- Do not look at or touch my body.
- When you sit, keep your legs together.
- Don't get too friendly with Tesshi. Try to get him and Saya together.
- Don't touch other boys.
- Don't touch the girls, either.

⟨To Mitsuha—Don'ts List Ver. 5⟩
- I told you before, don't waste my money. Remember?
- Don't be late for school or work. Learn how to get there already.
- Don't talk with an accent.
- Are you sneaking baths? I think I smell shampoo...
- Don't get cuddly with Tsukasa, you idiot. People will get the wrong idea.
- Don't get too friendly with Okudera-senpai, I'm begging you.

—But still... I grit my teeth reading another of Mitsuha's journal entries.

Reading Taki's entry in my diary, my blood starts to boil. Honestly, I swear, this is just completely...

That guy...
That girl...   is such a...!

You "tore up the court" playing basketball in gym?! That's not me at all! Not only that, what are you doing jumping and bouncing around in front of the boys?! Saya even yelled at me and told me to keep my chest and stomach and legs covered properly! Male gazes! Watch your skirt! This is very basic stuff!!

▼

Mitsuha, you twit, don't go scarfing down crazy-expensive cakes! You're freaking out Tsukasa and the other guys, and that's my money!

▼

It's your body eating them, Taki! Besides, I'm working at that restaurant, too! Plus, you're taking too many shifts. I can't do anything fun this way.

▼

That's because you keep burning through my money! And seriously, no matter what I do, I can't make those braided cords with your grandma!

▼

On the way home, Okudera-senpai and I stopped and had tea! I tried to buy hers for her, but she paid for mine instead. "Take me out when you graduate from high school," she said! Can you believe that? "That's a promise," I told her, all cool-like. Your relationship is blossoming, so, you're welcome. ♡

▼

Mitsuha, what the hell do you think you're doing?! Don't go messing with my relationships!

▼

Taki! What is this love letter?! Why is some guy I don't know confessing to me?! Why did you tell him you'd "think about it"?!

▼

Ha-ha. You aren't using your assets at all. Don'cha think you'd be more popular if you let me run your life?

▼

Don't get full of yourself! You don't even have a girlfriend!

▼

You don't have anybody, either!

▼

It's not that...
It's not that... I don't have one—I'm just not looking!

✳   ✳   ✳

That's Mitsuha's ringtone.

Meaning, I'm living in the country today, I think sleepily. Awesome. I'll get to put in some more time on the café project I'm working on with Teshigawara after school. Yeah, and also—

I sit up on the futon and look down at my body.

Mitsuha's pajamas have gotten really conservative lately. She used to sleep in a baggy nightshirt without a bra. This morning, though, she's wearing underwear that's kinda constricting and this shirt that's buttoned up all the way. There's no telling when we're gonna swap, so she's being careful. Well, I get that. I do. But.

I reach for her breasts. This is my body today. *Nothing wrong with touching my own body*, I think, just like always. Only. Except. But...

My hands pause, and I mutter quietly:

"...Guess I shouldn't."

The sliding door rattles open.

"......You really do like your boobs, don't you, Sis?"

That's all the little sister says before closing the sliding door. I watch her go...while kneading my breasts.

...This is okay, right? From on top of her clothes. Just a little.

∗   ∗   ∗

"Graaaaan. Why's the body of our shrine's god all the way out here?" Yotsuha whines.

Gran, who's walking in front of us, answers without turning around. "Thanks to Mayugorou, I don't know, either."

Mayugorou?

"…Who's that?" I whisper to Yotsuha, who's plodding along next to me.

"Huh? You dunno? He's famous."

Famous? I don't really get how these relationships work in the country.

The three Miyamizu women—me, the grandma, and Yotsuha— have been hiking mountain roads for almost an hour already. Today, they tell me, we're taking an offering up to the body of their shrine's god on top of the mountain. *These people are living in a folktale*, I think, thoroughly impressed.

The sun shining through the canopy of maple leaves dyes them bright red. The air is crisp and dry, and there's a strong scent of dead leaves in the pleasant wind. October. Who knows when it happened, but it's full autumn in this town now.

Come to think of it, I wonder how old this old lady is.

The thought comes to me gazing at the small back ahead of me. Even on this mountain trail, she's wearing traditional clothes. She's a surprisingly strong walker, but her back has a textbook stoop, and she's using a walking stick. I've never lived with an old person, so I can't even begin to guess her age or what kind of shape she's in.

"Hey, Grandma!"

I break into a run, then kneel in front of her, offering my back. After all, this little old lady is raising Mitsuha and her sister, and she always packs us really good lunches.

"Let me piggyback you. If you want…"

"Oh, may I?" Even as she speaks, she's happily lowering her

weight onto my back. I catch a distinct whiff of a mysterious fragrance I smelled once at somebody else's house a very long time ago. For a moment, I get a strange, warm feeling, as if this moment has happened before. The old lady weighs nothing.

"Grandma, you're way light— Whoa!"

The moment I stand, the added cargo buckles my (Mitsuha's) knees. Yotsuha hastily supports me, complaining, "Come on, Sis!" Come to think of it, Mitsuha's body is pretty flimsy and thin and light, too. Moving through the world this way...it's kinda amazing. The thought gets to me a bit.

"Mitsuha, Yotsuha."

I hear the old lady's voice over my shoulder, sounding serene.

"Are you familiar with *musubi*?"

"*Musubi*?"

Yotsuha asks the question from beside me. She's hugging my backpack to her stomach. Below us, through the gaps between the trees, I can see the whole round lake. We've climbed pretty high. Mitsuha's body is all sweaty from climbing with her grandma on her back.

"In the old language, our local guardian deity is called *Musubi*, 'creator of spirits.' It's a word with several very profound meanin's."

Guardian deity? Where'd this come from all of a sudden? Still, the old lady's voice is like something out of the *Manga Japan Folktales* program, and it's oddly persuasive.

"Did you know?" she starts again. "Joinin' threads is called *musubi*. Joinin' people is also *musubi*. The passage of time is *musubi*, too. They all use the same word. It's a name for our god, and the god's power. It describes the braided cords we make, divine acts, and the flow of time itself."

I can hear the murmur of running water. *Must be a stream around here*, I think.

"Comin' together to form a shape, twistin' and tanglin', sometimes comin' undone, breakin' off, then reunitin'. That's a braided cord. That's time. That's *musubi*."

Without really meaning to, I visualize a stream of clear water. It runs up against rocks and splits, mingles with others, joins up again, and, seen as a whole, it's all connected. I don't really understand what the old lady's saying, but I feel as if I've learned something very important. *Musubi*. Even after I wake up, I'll make sure to remember that word. Sweat drips off my chin, falling to the ground with a distinctive *plop*, and is absorbed into the dry mountain.

"Here, drink up."

We take a short break in the shade. The old lady hands me a thermos.

It's nothing big, just sweetened barley tea. Even so, it's shockingly good, and I drain two cups in a row. "C'mon! Me too!" Yotsuha pesters. This may be the best drink I've ever had.

"That's another *musubi*."

"Huh?"

As I hand the thermos to Yotsuha, I involuntarily look over at the old lady. She's sitting at the base of a tree.

"Puttin' anythin' in your body, whether it's water, rice, or sake, is also called *musubi*. Did you know that? What you put in your body binds to your soul, you see. And so, the offerin' we're makin' today is an important tradition meant to connect the god and humans to each other, a custom that the Miyamizu family has observed for centuries."

Before I notice, the trees end, and the lake town below us—now about the size of a sketchbook—is half-hidden beneath the clouds. When I look up, the wisps of cloud still overhead seem paper-thin, transparent and shining. They're flowing rapidly into the distance and dissolving in the strong wind. We're in a rocky area where only moss grows. We've finally reached the peak.

"I see it, I see it!"

Yotsuha's skipping around. I catch up to her and follow her gaze. Ahead, there's a crater-like basin about the size of an athletic field, as if the top of the mountain has been gouged out. The inside is a green, marshy area, and near its center stands a massive, solitary tree.

I'd never even imagined a view like this one, and I stare.

It's almost like a natural floating garden. You'd never be able to see it from the town. The boondocks are all kinds of awesome.

"This is the edge of the other side," the old lady says.

We've gone down to the basin floor, and there's a little brook flowing in front of us. The big tree is beyond.

"Other side?" Yotsuha and I say together.

"The hidden world, the next world."

The next world. Grandma's folktale voice strokes my back like a cold wind. My feet falter just a little. A sacred mountain, or a power spot, or a save point—whatever it is, the atmosphere saturating it really does seem to belong to some other world.

This better not be one of those places that doesn't let you leave once you go in.

"Yaaaay, it's the next world!"

Yotsuha whoops and splashes across the little stream. Kids are really something, all dumb and full of energy. Well, the weather's nice, and the wind and the brook are both peaceful. I'd probably be embarrassed later if I got cold feet over something like this. I take the old lady's hand so she won't get wet, and we cross the brook on the stepping-stones.

"In order to return to our world...," the old lady begins, suddenly sounding solemn, "you two must leave behind what's most precious to you."

"Huh?!" In spite of myself, my voice gets shrill.

"W-wait, Grandma—don't say that after we're already here!"

The old woman smiles at my protest, and her eyes squinch up. I can see the gaps where she's missing teeth, and it's really creepy.

"There's nothin' to fear. I meant the sake. Take it out," the old lady instructs, and both Yotsuha and I remove small urns from our backpacks. They're the kind of thing you tend to see on Shinto altars in people's houses. Made of glossy white ceramic, their rounded shapes are a few inches across, and they widen into a pedestal at the base. The lids are sealed with braided cords, and I can hear liquid splashing inside.

"Below the god's body," Grandma says, gazing at the enormous tree, "there's a little shrine. Offer them there. That sake is half of you, you see."

Half of Mitsuha.

I look at the urn in my hands. It's that special sake, the stuff she made by chewing up rice. This sake was made by "binding" rice and this body... And I'm the one offering it. Feeling awkward—like I'm about to score a goal off a pass from someone I've been fighting with—but at the same time strangely proud, I start toward the great tree.

This might be the first time I've heard real evening cicadas.

I know what they are because it's the sound effect they always use for evening in movies and games. Their melancholy, wavering song echoes all around me—everywhere—and it makes this whole experience seem a lot more movielike than an actual movie.

There's a loud rustling, and a flock of sparrows bursts out of the brush right in front of me. Having been under the impression that birds just hung out in trees, I'm startled, but Yotsuha runs after them, twirling around and around. She looks like she's having fun. We must be pretty close to the town—there are faint dinnertime smells on the wind. The idea that it's possible to so clearly distinguish the scents of everyday human life surprises me a little.

"It's already half-light."

Having completed the day's formal business, Yotsuha sounds relieved, like she's finally finished her homework. The evening sun lights up the girl and the old lady sidelong, like a spotlight. It's almost too picture-perfect.

"Whoa...!"

The sight of the village coming into view below us makes me exhale despite myself. I can see Mitsuha's entire town around the edge of the lake. Blue shadows have already engulfed the town itself, but the lake yawning beside reflects the red sky. On the hillsides here and there, pink evening mists are gathering. Dinner smoke rises from several houses, trailing high and thin, like smoke signals. The sparrows skimming through the air over the town gleam randomly, like motes of dust after school.

"Think we'll be able to see the comet soon?"

Yotsuha is searching the sky, blocking out the setting sun with her palm.

"Comet?"

Now that she mentions it, I remember they were talking about something like that on TV during breakfast, about how the comet's been close enough to be visible to the naked eye for a few days now and how, just after sunset today, we'd probably be able to see it if we looked diagonally above Venus.

"The comet..."

I say it aloud one more time. Out of nowhere, I feel as if I've forgotten something.

I narrow my eyes, searching the western sky, and find what I'm looking for right away. Above Venus, which is especially bright, I see the comet's shining blue tail. In the depths of my memory, something's trying to surface.

That's right. Once before, I...

That comet—

"...My, my. Mitsuha."

Before I know she's there, Grandma's peering up at me—into me. My shadow is reflected at the bottom of her deep black eyes.

"You're dreamin', aren't you?"

!

All of a sudden…

I wake up.

I've flung the sheet away, and it falls off the bed without a sound. My heart's pounding hard enough to raise my ribs (at least I think it is), but I can't hear my heartbeat. That's weird— But just after the thought forms, little by little, I start hearing my blood pumping. The morning sparrows outside the window, car engines, the rumble of trains. As if I'm finally remembering where I am, my ears begin taking in Tokyo.

"…Tears?"

I touch my cheek and find droplets of water on my fingertips.

Why? I don't know. I wipe my eyes with my palm. Even as I do, the twilight landscape from a moment ago and the old lady's words are disappearing, like water soaking into sand.

Tweedle.

By my pillow, my phone chirps.

I'm almost there. I'm looking forward to today. ♡

It's a Line message from Okudera-senpai.

Almost here? What's she talking about? …And then I gasp.

"Wait, did Mitsuha—? Not again!" Panicked, I dive into my phone and read Mitsuha's memo. "A date?!"

I bolt out of bed and get ready at top speed.

Date with Okudera-senpai in Roppongi tomorrow! She'll be waiting in front of Yotsuya Station at 10:30. It's a date I want to go on, but if I'm unlucky and it ends up being you, be grateful and enjoy it.

Fortunately, the place where we're meeting is nearby. I sprint flat out and arrive with ten minutes to spare. As I catch my breath, I check my phone to make sure. Okudera-senpai might not be here yet. Even though it's a weekend morning, the area around the station is still pretty lively.

I wipe away my sweat, straighten my jacket collar, and mutter "Mitsuha, you idiot" three times. Then, just in case, I start looking for Okudera-senpai.

...I'm on a date with *the* Okudera-senpai. Not only that, but as it happens, this is my first date ever. A first date with Okudera-senpai, who's like an idol, or an actress, or Miss Japan? Yeah, that's setting the bar fiendishly high. *Mitsuha, you moron. It's not too late yet, so I'm begging you, switch places with me!*

"Taaaki!"

"Waugh!"

A voice startles me from behind, and I give a really lame yell. Hastily, I turn around.

"Sorry. Did I keep you waiting?"

"No, I wasn't waiting! Uh, I mean, yes, I was! Or, no..."

What's with that question?! If I tell her I waited, I might make her feel bad, and if I tell her I wasn't waiting, I risk making her think I was late. Aaagh, what's the right answer?

"Um, I, er..."

Flustered, I look up. Okudera-senpai is standing right there, smiling at me.

"...!"

My eyes go wide. She's in black mules, a white flared miniskirt, and a black off-the-shoulder blouse. The monochrome outfit leaves her shoulders and legs dazzlingly exposed, and several gold accessories have been placed strategically, as if placing a careful seal on the charms of her skin. There's a large mocha-colored ribbon on her small white hat.

She looks incredibly sophisticated and incredibly pretty.

"…I just got here."

"Oh, good!" she laughs, sounding chipper.

"Shall we?"

She takes my arm… Ah, for a moment—just a moment—your breast touched my arm. I have a sudden, immediate urge to polish every window in this town.

"The conversation keeps dying…"

In the bathroom, I'm hanging my head real, real low. I feel like smashing it against the mirror.

Three hours into the date, and I'm already more exhausted than I've ever been in my life. I had no idea I was this bad with girls. No, that's not it. I hope that's not it. It's all Mitsuha's fault for throwing me into this situation unprepared. And more than anything, it's Okudera-senpai's fault for being too pretty.

I mean, everybody we pass stares at her with their mouths hanging open. Then they see me walking beside her and give me the stink-eye, like they're thinking, *What's that little punk doing there?* That's what it looks like to me, anyway.

Well, sure. Even I know I'm out of my league. Look, I didn't ask her out! I want to go around grabbing people's shoulders and making excuses for myself. Consequently, I have absolutely no idea what to talk about. Okudera-senpai can tell and tries starting conversations with me, but that makes me insanely uncomfortable, which makes it even harder to talk. It's a vicious cycle.

Dammit, Mitsuha, what do you and Okudera-senpai usually talk about?!

Hoping for a lifeline, I open my phone and check Mitsuha's memo.

…That said, I bet you've never been on a date before.

And so, below, I've put together a collection of handpicked links, just for you!

"Whoa, seriously?!"

Look at that! She's practically a god! I open the links as if clinging to them for dear life.

Link 1: How I gots me a girlfriend even tho I has a communication disorder

Link 2: Conversation skills for the person who's never, ever been the tiniest bit popular!

Link 3: You won't make 'em sick anymore! A feature on texts they'll love

…Somehow I get the feeling she's selling me way, way short.

Walking through the art museum, I'm finally feeling a little relieved.

I'm not particularly interested in the photo exhibit, which is titled *Nostalgia*, but it's great to be somewhere it isn't weird not to talk. Okudera-senpai is five feet ahead of me, strolling slowly, placidly gazing at the pictures.

Furano, Tsugaru, Sanriku, Rikuzen, Aizu, Shinshu… The exhibition is divided regionally, but all the rustic scenery looks the same to me. I don't know the right way to appreciate photos, but about the only differences I can make out are whether the background is mountains or ocean and whether it's summer or winter. The houses and train stations and roads and people all seem oddly similar. I guess rural Japan probably looks like this no matter where you go. In that case, the districts in Tokyo have a lot more personality. "Shibuya and Ikebukuro," for example, or "Akasaka and Kichijouji," or "Meguro and Tachikawa."

Even so, in the section labeled *Hida*, my feet stop all by themselves.

This one is different from the others.

Well, no. The photos still look similar, but I know this place—the contours of the mountains, the curve of the road, the size of the lake, the shape of the red shrine gates, the layout of the fields. I just know, the way you can always pick out your own shoes from a mess of scattered sneakers without even trying. I never actually went to visit relatives in the country during summer vacations when I was a kid, but that's what this feels like. I'm having a surreal, powerful sense of déjà vu about the place. This is—

"Taki?"

When I turn toward the voice, Okudera-senpai is standing beside me. For a second, I forgot she existed.

"You know, Taki," she says with an even smile, "you seem like a different person today."

She executes a beautiful turn, like a model, and strides away, leaving me behind.

I blew it.

All I did today was trudge through the date Mitsuha planned like the whole thing had been a chore. I just kept coming up with excuses and didn't even consider what Okudera-senpai, who was right there with me, might be feeling. Even though I (well, Mitsuha) was the one who'd invited her. Even though I should've been ecstatic just to get to spend time with her. Even though I've spent my whole life hoping for a miraculous day exactly like this.

From the pedestrian bridge, I have a clear view of the cluster of Roppongi buildings we just left. Hundreds of windows shine golden in the evening sun. My eyes go back to Okudera-senpai ahead of me. She's not saying a word.

Her hair gleams, and her hat and clothes look brand new. Today, at least, she might have gone to all that trouble just for me. The thought makes my throat tighten. I feel like the oxygen's suddenly thinned, and it's hard to breathe. I grope for words as if desperately flailing for the surface of the ocean.

"Um, Okudera-senpai?"

She doesn't turn.

"...Are you hungry? We could go get dinner somewhere—"

"Why don't we call it a day instead?" she suggests with the tone of a patient teacher.

"Okay."

On the spur of the moment, I say something really boneheaded. Okudera-senpai has finally turned around, but her expression, fading into the evening sun—I can't see it clearly.

"Taki... Forgive me if I'm wrong, all right?"

"Sure."

"A long time ago, you liked me a little bit, didn't you?"

"Huh?!" She knew?! How?!

"And now there's someone else you like, isn't there?"

"Huuuuuuuh?!" I gush sweat as if I've suddenly teleported into a tropical rain forest. "N-no, there isn't!"

"Really?"

"Th-there isn't! There's absolutely nobody like that!"

"I wonder..."

Okudera-senpai examines my face skeptically. Somebody else I like? No, there's nobody like that. I'm pretty sure there isn't. Just for a moment, *her* long hair and the softness of her breasts flicker through my mind but vanish almost immediately.

"Well, never mind."

Her tone is bright and clear, and her face recedes.

"Huh?"

"Thank you for today. I'll see you at work."

Okudera-senpai flutters a hand at me, then simply walks away, leaving me behind. Mechanically, I open my mouth. Close it. Open it again. Even so, no words come out, and while I'm doing that,

Okudera-senpai's back descends from the pedestrian bridge and disappears into the crowd in front of the station.

I gaze at the evening sun, feeling as if I've been abandoned on the edge of summer. There are no breaks in the cars streaming under the pedestrian bridge, and after I've been listening to them for a while, I start feeling as though I'm on a real bridge, over a river. The late sun is as weak as a flashlight, and it's disappearing behind the water tank on top of a mixed-use building. I focus on it the entire time, intently, as if trying to reclaim something.

It feels like there are other things I should be doing, but I can't think of anything specific. I just want to go to Mitsuha's town again, fast. Becoming Mitsuha means talking to her, too. When we're swapped, at the same time, we're connected in some special way. We're trading experiences. We're bound together the way her grandma was talking about. If I turn into Mitsuha, I think I'll be able to talk about what happened today. I want to joke around with her. *"That's why you're not popular, you know." "It's your fault for promising stuff without checking first."*

I open the memo on my phone. There's more to Mitsuha's note.

> **The comet should be visible just about the time the date ends.**
>
> **Eeeeee, how romantic! I can't wait for tomorrow. ♡**
>
> **Whether it's me or you, let's do our best on the date!**

Comet?

I look up at the sky. The last traces of the sunset are already gone. A few of the brightest stars are out, and a jet's flying past, humming faintly, but that's it. Needless to say, there's no comet.

"What's she talking about?" I mutter quietly.

If a comet people could actually see was passing, it would've been pretty big news. Maybe Mitsuha got mixed up.

Abruptly, my heart twinges uneasily in its darkest recesses.

Something's trying to surface in my mind.

I flip through the phone and pull up Mitsuha's cell number, staring at those eleven digits. Back when we first started swapping, I tried calling this number several times, but for some reason, it never went through. I touch it with a fingertip. The "calling" sound plays. Then I hear a voice from the speaker:

"The number you have dialed is unavailable. Either the number is not in service or the unit is turned off or out of range…"

I pull the phone away from my ear and press END CALL.

So calls really don't get through. Well, whatever. I'll just tell her about this train wreck of a day next time we swap. I'll ask her about the comet, too. We'll switch tomorrow or the day after, anyway. With that thought, I finally descend the pedestrian bridge. There's a pale, smooth half-moon overhead, all alone, as if someone forgot it there.

But after that, Mitsuha and I never swapped again.

Chapter Four

The Search

I move my pencil tirelessly.

Carbon particles blend into the paper fibers, lines accumulate, and the once-white sketchbook grows darker and darker. Even so, I haven't managed to completely capture the sights in my memory.

Every morning, I take the train to school during the commuter rush. I sit through boring classes. I eat lunch with Tsukasa and Takagi. I walk through town, looking up at the sky. Somewhere along the way, its blue has grown a little deeper. Bit by bit, the trees lining the streets begin to change color.

In my room at night, I draw. On my desk, there's a stack of mountain guidebooks I borrowed from the library. I search the ranges of Hida on my smartphone. I look for ridgelines that match the ones I remember. I keep my pencil in motion, trying to copy them down onto paper somehow.

Some days, rain falls, smelling like asphalt. Some days shine with billowing clouds reminiscent of sheep. Some days, strong winds blow, peppering Tokyo with yellow sand. Every morning, I ride crowded trains to school. I go to my part-time job. Sometimes, Okudera-senpai and I work the same shift. I do my best to look her in the eye, to smile properly, to talk normally. I think, very firmly, that I want to be fair to everyone.

Some nights are still as hot and humid as midsummer, while others are chilly enough that I wear my track jacket. No matter the temperature, when I'm drawing, I get so hot it feels like I have a blanket wrapped around my head. Sweat plops audibly onto my sketchbook. It blurs the lines I've drawn. Even so, the sights of the town I saw as Mitsuha are taking shape, coming together, bit by bit.

On the way home from school, on the way home from work, I skip the train and take long walks. The scenery of Tokyo changes by the day. Before I know it, there are rows of enormous cranes in Shinjuku and the Outer Garden area around Meiji Shrine and Yotsuya, at the foot of the Benkei Bridge and partway up Anchinzaka Hill. Little by little, steel frames and glass stretch up toward the sky. Beyond them, there's a blank, waning half-moon.

Finally, I finish several drawings of the lake town.
This weekend, I'll head out.
Having made that resolution, I feel the tension drain from my stiff body for the first time in a long while. Even standing up seems like too much work, so I slump over my desk.

Just before I fall asleep, I wish hard, the way I always do…
…but I still don't wake up as Mitsuha.

I've packed three days' worth of underwear and my sketchbook in my backpack. Thinking it might be a little cold there, I put on a thick jacket with a deep hood. I wind my lucky friendship bracelet around my wrist as usual, then leave the condo.

It's earlier than I generally leave for school, so the train's empty, although Tokyo Station is still teeming with people. I line up after some foreigners with wheeled suitcases, buy a Shinkansen ticket to Nagoya from the automatic ticket machine, and head for the Tokaido Shinkansen turnstile.

I don't believe my eyes.

"Wha...? Why are you here?!"

Okudera-senpai and Tsukasa are standing together beside a pillar right in front of me. Okudera-senpai grins.

"Eh-heh-heh. Well, here I am!"

...Well, here you are? What are you, the heroine of some cutesy anime?!

I glare at Tsukasa. He looks back at me, his expression bland as if to say, *Is there a problem?*

"Tsukasa, you jerk! I asked you to give me an alibi for my dad and to cover my shift at work, remember?!"

I berate Tsukasa, who's in the seat next to mine, under my breath. Almost all the unreserved seats on the bullet train are filled with businessmen in suits.

"Takagi's covering for you at work," he says smoothly, displaying his phone.

"Leave it to me!" Takagi flashes a breezy thumbs-up in the video. *"Buy me a meal, though."*

"Every single friggin' one of you...," I mutter sourly.

Asking Tsukasa was a mistake. I was planning to skip school today and spend the weekend—Friday, Saturday, and Sunday—in Hida. I went to Tsukasa yesterday and begged him for help, telling him that something had come up and I absolutely had to go see a friend, asking him to not ask questions and just let me use him as an excuse while I was gone.

"I came because I was worried about you," Tsukasa says without a hint of penitence. "I couldn't just leave you alone, could I? What are you gonna do if it turns out to be a badger game?"

"A badger what?"

What's he talking about? My eyebrows knit, and Okudera-senpai, who's sitting on Tsukasa's opposite side, leans in.

"You're going to see a friend you met online, aren't you, Taki?"

"Huh? No, the online thing was just an excuse, and, uh…" Yesterday, Tsukasa was really persistent about asking who I was visiting, so I vagued things up and told him it was somebody I'd met on a social networking site.

Tsukasa gravely informs Okudera-senpai, "Frankly, I suspect it's a dating site."

I nearly do a spit take.

"It is not!"

"You've seemed really off lately, you know." Looking concerned, Tsukasa extends a box of Pocky to me. "We'll hang back and watch from a distance."

"What am I, a grade-schooler?!" I demand, lashing out.

Okudera-senpai watches me knowingly. She's absolutely got the wrong idea about this, too.

This is gonna be one rough trip, I think dismally.

"*Approaching Nagoya*," a lazy voice announces over the train's loudspeaker.

The exchanges with Mitsuha started out of the blue one day and ended just as suddenly. No matter how much thought I gave it, I couldn't figure out why. After several weeks, it got harder to shake the suspicion they might just have been a string of extremely vivid dreams.

I've got proof, though. I can't believe that the journal entries Mitsuha left on my phone came out of my own head. That date with Okudera-senpai could never have happened if I'd been myself. I'm convinced Mitsuha's a real girl. Her body heat, her pulse, the way she breathes, her voice, the red light dawning over her closed eyes, the vibrant sounds in her ears—I felt all of that myself. Experiencing her life was so intense, it convinced me, *If she isn't alive, then nothing is.* Mitsuha is real.

Because of that, the abrupt way it ended is making me oddly uneasy. Something might have happened to her. Maybe she came down with a fever. Maybe there was some sort of accident. Even if I'm overthinking things, at the very least, she's bound to be worried about the situation, too. That's why I decided to go see her in person. But...

"...Excuse me? You don't actually know where she is?"

We're in a four-person box seat on the express train *Hida*. Okudera-senpai sounds incredulous, stuffing her face with a box lunch she picked up at the station.

"...Right."

"Your only clue is what the town looks like? You can't even contact this girl? Are you kidding me?!"

I didn't ask her to come with me. How come I'm getting blamed? I look at Tsukasa, willing him to say something. He does, swallowing a bite of miso cutlet.

"You are an abysmal tour planner."

"This isn't a tour!"

I lose it for a second. These two think they're on some kind of field trip. I can read their expressions clearly. *There's just no help for this child.* Why are they acting all superior, anyway?

"Well, never mind," Okudera-senpai says. Unexpectedly, she smiles, throwing out her chest. "Don't you worry, Taki. We'll help you look."

"Eeeee, it's so cuuuute! Taki, look at this, looook!"

At the local station we finally reached after noon, Okudera-senpai gushes over the area's laid-back mascot. It's a full-body plush cow costume wearing a station employee cap. The camera on Tsukasa's phone fires off click after click in the little terminal.

"You guys are in the way."

As I glare at the local map posted in the station, I'm even more convinced that these two are going to be no help whatsoever. I'll just have to find her myself.

The plan goes like this:

Since I don't know exactly where Mitsuha's town is, we'll take the train to a spot that seems close to the scenery in my memory. From that point, all we'll have to go on will be the landscape sketches I drew. We'll go around showing the drawings to residents, asking if anyone recognizes them, slowly working our way north along the local line. There's a railroad crossing in one of the scenes I remember, so following the tracks should work.

It's a really vague approach, to the point where I can't really call it a "plan" at all, but I couldn't think of any other way. Besides, there can't be that many towns built around lakes. I'm convinced I'll probably find some kind of hint by tonight, though I've got no grounds for thinking that.

Psyching myself up, I take a confident first step, heading out to talk to the driver of the lone taxi parked outside the station.

"…This isn't gonna work…"

I'm slumped at a bus stop, my head drooping.

All the confidence I had when we started asking around has completely caved.

After that first taxi driver gave me a blunt "N-nope, dunno," we tried police boxes, convenience stores, souvenir shops, guest houses, diners, and everyone from farmers to grade-school kids, oblivious to how we probably looked, but our results were solidly negative. The fact that there was only one local train every two hours made it hard for us to get around, so we thought we'd try asking people on the bus. We boarded in high spirits but were the only passengers. I didn't even feel like asking the driver at that point, and the last stop was way out in the middle of nowhere, with no houses anywhere in sight. The whole time, Tsukasa and Okudera-senpai cheerfully made the most of their day trip, playing word games, cards, phone games, variations on rock-paper-scissors, and eating snacks. Eventually, they ended up on either side of me on the bus, leaning against my shoulders and dozing peacefully.

Now, as the two of them guzzle cola in front of the bus stop, I sigh. They hear it and react together.

"Oh, come on, Taki! You're giving up already?!"

"What about all our hard work?!"

I heave another sigh, so deep it almost brings my lungs up with it. Okudera-senpai's wearing oddly gung-ho clothes meant for serious hiking. In contrast, Tsukasa's in chinos like he's just strolling around the neighborhood. At this point, both outfits really irritate me.

"You guys have been zero help…"

They both look innocent, as if to say, *Oh, really?*

"I'll have a Takayama ramen."

"One Takayama ramen here."

"Uh, okay, then I'll have the same, too."

"You betcha. Three ramen!" says the middle-aged lady cheerily.

On our fruitless way to the next (abnormally distant) station, we found a ramen shop that was miraculously open and made a beeline inside. When the lady wearing a triangular kerchief told us, "C'mon in," her smile seemed a beacon, not unlike the appearance of a long-awaited search party when you're lost.

The ramen's good, too. Contrary to its name, it's perfectly ordinary ramen (I thought it might have Hida beef on top, but it was regular braised pork), but as soon as I eat the noodles and veggies, I can feel my body recharging. After draining the soup bowl dry and drinking two cups of water, I finally take a breather.

"Do you think we'll be able to get back to Tokyo today?" I ask Tsukasa.

"Hmm… I don't know. We may be cutting it close. Want me to check?"

Tsukasa apparently didn't expect this but nevertheless pulls out his phone and starts looking up how to get home.

"Thanks," I tell him.

"Taki, you're sure that's all right?" Okudera-senpai asks.

She's across the table from me and hasn't finished eating yet. I'm not immediately sure how to answer, so I look out the window. The sun's just barely caught on the edge of the mountains, shining peacefully over the fields along the prefectural highway.

"I can't explain it, but it's starting to feel like I'm on the wrong track," I mutter, half to myself. It might be better to go back to Tokyo and rework my strategy. It would be one thing if I had photos, but expecting to find the town with sketches like these might have been asking too much. At least, that's how it starts to seem when I pick up my sketchbook and gaze at it. It's a completely ordinary country town, with the sort of houses you see everywhere scattered around a round lake. Even though it felt so solid to me when I finished drawing it, it looks like an anonymous, mediocre landscape now.

"That's old Itomori, ain't it?"

"Huh?" I turn around and see the lady's apron. She's pouring water into my empty cup.

"Did you draw that, son? Say, can I have a look?" She takes the sketchbook from me. "This is a real good picture. Hon, c'mere a sec!"

The woman shouts back toward the kitchen. The three of us watch her, mouths agape.

The ramen shop owner comes out of the kitchen and considers the sketch, smiling a little. "Oh, yeah. That was Itomori, for sure. Takes me back…"

"My man's from Itomori, you see."

Itomori?

Suddenly, I remember. I start up out of my chair.

"Itomori... Yeah, Itomori! Of course, why couldn't I remember that? It's Itomori! It's near here, isn't it?!"

The couple looks mystified, exchanging perplexed glances. The man opens his mouth.

"Kid... You know about Itomori, don't you? That's where—"

Tsukasa interrupts loudly. "Itomori?! Taki, don't tell me—"

"What, wait—? You mean, the one where the comet...?!"

Even Okudera-senpai speaks up, eyes wide.

"Huh......?"

I don't understand what's going on and look around at the others. They're all watching me dubiously. The shadow of something that's been trying to surface in my mind this whole time rustles stealthily, growing more and more ominous.

The cry of a kite trails through the atmosphere, lonely enough to freeze the blood.

A row of DO NOT ENTER barricades extends as far as the eye can see, throwing long shadows over the cracked asphalt.

A sign with vines tangled around it reads, IN ACCORDANCE WITH THE DISASTER COUNTERMEASURES BASIC ACT, THIS AREA IS OFF-LIMITS. KEEP OUT.—RECONSTRUCTION AGENCY.

And below me lies Itomori, devastated by some unimaginable force and mostly swallowed up by the lake.

"...Is this really the place?"

Okudera-senpai walks up behind me, her voice trembling. Without waiting for me to respond, Tsukasa answers, sounding desperately cheerful.

"It can't be! Like I've been saying, Taki's confused."

"...This is it."

I tear my eyes away from the ruins below me, scanning my surroundings.

"It isn't just the town. I remember this schoolyard, the

mountains around us, the high school… I remember all of it perfectly!"

I have to shout the words to convince myself. Behind us is the school building, black and sooty, with some of its windows broken. We're standing on the grounds of Itomori High School, looking out across the lake.

"So you're saying this is the town you were looking for? The one where your friend online lives?" Tsukasa shouts, that parched smile still clinging to his voice.

"That's not even possible! That disaster was three years ago. Hundreds of people died! You remember it, right, Taki?!"

At that, I finally turn toward Tsukasa.

"…Died?"

I meant to look at his face, but my gaze goes right through him, then through the high school behind him, only to dissipate into the distance. I know I must be looking at something, but there's nothing there.

"Three years ago…she died?"

Abruptly, I remember.

The comet I saw over Tokyo three years earlier. Countless shooting stars falling through the western sky. I thought it was beautiful, like something out of a dream. I got all excited about it.

That's when she died?

Don't.

I can't acknowledge that.

I search for words. For proof.

"That can't be true… I mean, look, I've got the journal entries she wrote."

I retrieve my phone out of my pocket. Spurred on by the inane fear that the battery will die forever if I take too long, I flip through it in a panic and pull up Mitsuha's journal entries. They're really there.

"…!"

I rub my eyes, hard. For a moment, the letters seemed to writhe.

"Wha…?"

First one letter, then another.

The words Mitsuha wrote begin dissolving into meaningless symbols. Before long, the text flickers like a candle flame, and then it's gone. One by one, her entries disappear entirely. It's as though an invisible man is holding down DELETE. As I watch, all her sentences vanish.

"Why…?" I ask very quietly.

The kite's cry echoes again, high and distant.

Three years ago in October, right around this time of year, Tiamat, a comet with a solar orbital period of twelve hundred years, made its closest approach to Earth. It was a satellite on a grand scale; its super-long orbital period put Halley's Comet's seventy-six to shame, and it had an orbital radius of 10.4 billion miles. Not only that, but it was projected to pass within roughly seventy-five thousand miles of Earth—closer than the moon. The tail of this shining blue comet would stream across the dome of the night sky for the first time in twelve hundred years. The mood of the entire world was festive as it welcomed Comet Tiamat.

Until the very moment it happened, no one anticipated that the comet's nucleus would split in Earth's vicinity. Or that a rocky mass about 130 feet in diameter was buried in its icy core. The comet fragment became a meteorite, plummeting to Earth at the devastating speed of almost twenty miles per second. Tragically, it struck Japan—a residential area called Itomori.

The town happened to be holding its autumn festival that day. The collision occurred at 8:42 PM. The point of impact was near Miyamizu Shrine, which must have been lined with festival stalls and teeming with people.

The meteorite instantly destroyed a wide area, centered on the shrine. The destruction wasn't limited to houses and the forest. The impact gouged a huge hole in the ground, forming a crater nearly half a mile across. One second later, magnitude 4.8 tremors rocked locations three miles away. Fifteen seconds later, the blast wind tore through, inflicting enormous damage on the greater part of the town. The final death toll was more than five hundred, a third of the town's population. Itomori became the site of the worst meteorite disaster in human history.

Since the crater had formed right beside Itomori Lake, water rushed in, ultimately creating a gourd-shaped body of water, New Itomori Lake.

Damage to the southern side of the town was relatively light, but even the thousand or so residents who escaped injury moved away, one after another. In less than a year, the town was having trouble functioning as a municipality. Fourteen months after the meteorite fell, for all intents and purposes, Itomori was gone.

—These are textbook facts, and of course, I knew most of them already. Three years ago, I was in middle school. I remember actually watching Comet Tiamat from a hill in my neighborhood.

…But that's weird.

It doesn't make sense.

I lived in Itomori as Mitsuha, several times, right up until last month.

That means that what I saw, the place where she lived, wasn't Itomori.

The comet and my swapping with Mitsuha had nothing to do with each other.

It'd be normal to think that. It's what I want to think.

However, paging through books in this city library near Itomori, I'm hopelessly confused. For a while now, in the deepest corner of my mind, someone's been whispering, *This is where you were.*

Vanished Itomori—Complete Records
Itomori—The Village That Sank in a Night
The Tragedy of Comet Tiamat

I flip through tome after tome with titles like these. The photos of bygone days in Itomori unmistakably show places I've been. This is the grade school Yotsuha goes to. Miyamizu Shrine is where their grandma is the chief priestess. This pointlessly big parking lot, the two snack bars right next to each other, the convenience store that looks like a barn, the little railroad crossing on the mountain road, and of course Itomori High School... At this point, I recognize all of them clearly. Seeing those ruined streets with my own eyes has sharpened my memories.

It's hard to breathe. My heart is struggling, beating irregularly, and refuses to calm down.

It feels as though the vivid photos are silently absorbing the air and any sense of reality.

Itomori High—Final Sports Festival

The photo above the caption shows high schoolers in the middle of a three-legged race. The pair on the end seems familiar. One has straight-cut bangs and braids. The other girl's hair is bound up with an orange cord.

The air gets even thinner.

I feel as though hot blood is oozing down the back of my neck, but when I wipe it away with my hand, it's transparent sweat.

"—Taki."

I look up. Tsukasa and Okudera-senpai are standing there. They hand me a single book. Foil letters in a weighty font are stamped on its thick cover:

Itomori Comet Disaster　List and Catalog of Victims

I turn the pages. The victims' names and addresses are given by district. I run my finger down them. I keep turning pages. Finally, my finger stops on names I recognize.

Teshigawara, Katsuhiko (17)
Natori, Sayaka (17)

"Teshigawara and Saya…"

As I murmur, I hear Tsukasa and Okudera-senpai suck in their breath.

Then I find the names that prove it all.

Miyamizu, Hitoha (82)
Miyamizu, Mitsuha (17)
Miyamizu, Yotsuha (9)

The other two peer over my shoulder at the list.

"That's her……? It has to be some kind of mistake! I mean, she's—" Okudera-senpai sounds as if she might burst into tears. "She's been dead for three years."

Trying to deny her words, I shout, "Just two or three weeks ago, she—!" It's hard to breathe. I inhale desperately and continue. This time, it comes out as a whisper. "She told me we'd be able to see the comet……"

I somehow manage to tear my eyes away from the letters that spell out *Mitsuha*.

"So…!"

When I raise my head, my face is reflected in the dark window in front of me. *Who are you?* I think, out of nowhere.

From deep in my mind, very far away, I hear a hoarse voice. *"…My, my. You're—"*

"You're dreamin', aren't you?"

A dream? I'm drowning in a wave of confusion.

What…

...in the world...
...am I doing?

In the next room, I can hear the sounds of a dinner party.

Someone says something, there's a burst of laughter, and then applause echoes like a downpour. It's been happening over and over for a while now. I strain my ears, wondering what sort of group they are. No matter how hard I listen, though, I can't make out a single word. All I can tell is that they're speaking Japanese.

Thunk! There's a loud noise, and the next thing I know, I'm slumped over with my head on the desk. I must've hit my forehead; a dull pain follows a little later. I'm dead tired.

No matter how much I read the reduced-size editions of old newspapers and magazine back issues, I can't seem to get the text into my head anymore. I've checked my phone several times, but not one of her journal entries is on it. Every trace is gone.

With my head still down, I open my eyes. Glaring at the desk a fraction of an inch in front of me, I try putting into words the conclusion I've reached over the past few hours.

"It was all just a dream, and..."

Do I want to believe that or not?

"The scenery looked familiar because I subconsciously remembered the news from three years ago. Meaning, she was..."

What was she?

"...A ghost? Or, no... It was all a..."

All...my...

"...Delusion?"

With a start, I raise my head.

Something's disappearing.

Her—

"What was her name…?"

Tap, tap, comes a sudden knock, and the thin wooden door opens.

"Tsukasa says he's going down to take a bath."

Okudera-senpai enters wearing one of the inn's light robes. The atmosphere in the room, which had seemed cold and isolated, suddenly softens. I feel terribly relieved.

"Uh, Okudera-senpai?"

I get up from my chair. She's crouched down in front of her backpack.

"I've been saying all sorts of weird stuff… I'm sorry about today."

Zipping her backpack as if carefully sealing something away, Okudera-senpai stands. Somehow she seems to move in slow motion.

"…It's fine," she says, shaking her head with a faint smile.

"I'm sorry we could only get one room."

"Tsukasa said the same thing to me downstairs," Okudera-senpai chuckles. We're sitting facing each other across the little table by the window.

"I don't mind a bit. They say a group just happened to be staying here tonight, so they don't have any rooms to spare. The man who runs the inn said it's a teachers' union social."

Then she laughingly tells me how they treated her to Asian pears in the lounge after she got out of the bath. She's the sort of person who makes everyone want to give her something. The scent of the inn's shampoo reaches me, like a rare perfume from a distant, foreign land.

"Look at that. Itomori used to make braided cords. How pretty," Okudera-senpai murmurs, flipping through a volume of local Itomori materials. It's one of the books I borrowed from the library.

"My mother wears kimonos sometimes, so we have several of these at home. Oh, say…"

Lifting my teacup, my hand pauses. She's examining my right wrist.

"That one on your wrist, Taki. Is that a braided cord?"

"Oh, this is…"

I set the cup down on the table and consider my arm. This is my good-luck charm: a vivid orange cord, thicker than a thread, wound around my wrist.

…Huh?

Isn't this—?

"I think somebody gave it to me a long time ago. I wear it sometimes, for good luck…"

The deepest part of my mind prickles again.

"Who was it?" I murmur.

I can't remember.

Still, if I follow this cord, it feels like I'll find something.

"…You, too, Taki."

The gentle voice makes me raise my head to see concern on Okudera-senpai's face. "Why don't you go take a bath?"

"A bath… Right…"

But almost immediately my attention returns to the braided cord. I feel as though I'll lose something forever if I let go here, and I desperately ransack my memories. The dinner party is over, though I don't know when it ended. The quiet song of autumn insects fills the room.

"Somebody who made braided cords told me something once."

Whose voice is that? It's kind and hoarse and tranquil. Like something from a folktale.

"They said that cords are the flow of time itself. They twist and tangle, come apart and reunite. They said that's time. That's…"

A mountain in autumn. The sound of a brook. The smell of water. The taste of sweet barley tea.

"That's *musubi*—"

The scene bursts into my mind.

The body of the god on top of the mountain. The sake we offered to it.

"…That place…!"

I pull a map out from under the pile of books and open it. It's a map of Itomori from three years ago that I found in a small independent shop, covered in dust. The topography from back when there was just one lake. The place where we offered the sake should be far outside the area the meteorite destroyed.

If I go there… If that sake's there…

I pick up my pencil, searching for a landform that looks likely. It was way north of the shrine, a place like a caldera. Desperately, I try to find something along those lines.

I might be hearing Okudera-senpai's voice, distantly, but by now, I can't tear my eyes off the map.

…ki… Taki.

Somebody's calling my name. It's a girl's voice.

"Taki, Taki."

Her voice is earnest, pleading, as if she's about to cry. A voice trembling with loneliness, like the glimmer of distant stars.

"Don't you remember me?"

I wake up.

…That's right. I'm at an inn. I've been sleeping slumped over the table by the window. I can sense Tsukasa and Okudera-senpai beyond the sliding door, asleep on their futons. The room is strangely quiet. I can't hear any insects or cars. The wind isn't blowing, either.

I sit up. The rustle of my clothes is loud enough to startle me. Outside the window, the world is just beginning to shake off the darkness.

I look at the cord on my wrist. The faint echoes of the girl's voice linger in my ears.

—*Who are you?* I ask. I don't even know her name.

Naturally, there's no answer.

But, well, that's all right.

> Okudera-senpai and Tsukasa—
>
> There's a place I need to check, no matter what.
> Please go back to Tokyo ahead of me. I'm sorry for
> being selfish. I swear I'll come back later. Thanks.
>   —Taki

I write a note. As an afterthought, I take a five-thousand-yen bill out of my wallet and put it under a teacup along with the memo.

We've never met, but I'm about to come looking for you.

✳ ✳ ✳

He's gruff and doesn't say much, but he's a really nice guy, I think, studying the sinewy hands on the steering wheel beside me.

It's the man from the ramen shop. He's the one who took us to Itomori High School yesterday, and to the city library. I called him really early this morning, and he still did me a favor and brought the car over. If this hadn't worked, I was planning to hitchhike, but I can't imagine any cars would've given me a ride to a ruined, abandoned town. I'm seriously lucky I met this guy in Hida.

From the passenger-side window, I have a view down to the edge of New Itomori Lake. Half-demolished houses and broken asphalt languish in the water. Even a good ways offshore, I can see telephone poles and iron beams jutting out of the lake. It should be a very disconcerting sight, but I must have gotten used to seeing it on TV and in photos, because I start feeling as if the place has always been like this. For that reason, I don't really know how to process what I'm seeing. Should I get mad, grieve, get scared, or lament my own helplessness? The reality of losing an entire town is probably too much for ordinary people to get their heads around. I give up searching for meaning in the scene and turn my eyes to the sky. Gray clouds hang over our heads, as if the gods have set an enormous lid there.

We travel north along the lake, and when the car can't go any higher, the man sets the parking brake.

"Looks like rain," he mutters, glancing up through the windshield. "This mountain ain't real steep, but don't push your luck. If anythin' happens, you call us."

"Yessir."

"Also, here—" He holds out a big lunch box to me. "Eat this up top."

Automatically, I accept it with both hands. It's heavy.

"Th-thank you very much…"

…For everything. Seriously. Why would you do so much for me? Oh yeah, and the ramen was super good. I can't make any of the words come out the way I want them to—all I manage is a tiny "Thanks. Really." The guy smiles slightly, takes out a cigarette, and lights up.

"I dunno what's goin' on with you," he says, exhaling smoke. "But that picture of Itomori you made. That was good."

There's a lump in my throat. Distant thunder rumbles softly.

I'm walking up a path to the shrine that's as vague as a deer track.

Sometimes I stop to check the destination I've marked on the map against the GPS on my phone. It's all right—I'm getting closer. The surrounding scenery looks sort of familiar, but I've climbed this mountain only once, in a dream. I'm not very sure about it. That means, for now, all I can do is follow the map.

After I got out of the car, I bowed low and stayed that way until my ride was completely out of sight. As I did, I thought about

Tsukasa and Okudera-senpai, too. In the end, this guy and those two came all the way out here because they were worried about me. I must've looked really pathetic. I bet they thought I was about to cry the whole time. I was probably so aggressively distracted that, even if they wanted to ditch me, they couldn't.

I can't keep acting like that forever. I can't keep taking advantage of the help people offer me, I think firmly, gazing at New Itomori Lake through the gaps in the trees.

Suddenly, a big raindrop hits my face. The leaves around me start to rustle and shake. I pull up my hood and break into a run.

The rain keeps falling, pouring down with enough force to carve the dirt away.

The temperature's falling rapidly, absorbed by the rain. I can feel it on my skin.

I eat my lunch in a little cave while waiting for the weather to let up. There are three big rice balls the size of my fist and lots of side dishes. The thick-sliced braised pork and bean sprouts stir-fried in sesame oil make it look like such a stereotypical ramen-shop lunch that it's funny. My body shakes with cold, but as I eat, I gradually warm up again. Chewing the grains of rice and swallowing, I can sense exactly where my throat and stomach are.

This is musubi, I think.

"Putting anything in your body, whether it's water, rice, or sake, is also called musubi. *What you put in your body binds to your soul, you see."*

That day, I decided I'd remember those words even after I woke up. I say it aloud:

"…They twist and tangle, sometimes come undone, and reunite. That's *musubi*. That's time."

I look at the cord on my wrist.

It hasn't worn through yet. The connection is still there.

*   *   *

Before I know it, the trees have vanished, and I'm in a mossy, rocky area. Below me, I can see fragments of the gourd-shaped lake through gaps in the thick clouds. I've finally reached the peak.

"…It's there!"

Sure enough, beyond me, there's the crater-shaped basin and the giant sacred tree.

"It's really there! It wasn't a dream!"

The rain has subsided to a drizzle, dripping down my cheeks like tears. I scrub roughly at my face with my sleeve, then start down the slope into the caldera.

In front of me, what was a little stream in my memories is now a decent-size pond. Is it swollen from the rain, or has enough time passed since that dream that the landscape changed? Either way, the great tree stands several dozen yards away on the other side.

This is the edge of the next world.

I remember somebody saying that to me once.

Does that make this the Sanzu River?

I step into the water. There's a big, echoing splash, as if I've stuck my foot into a bathtub, and I realize, belatedly, that this basin is unnaturally quiet. The heavy water is above my knees, and every step I take makes a loud sloshing sound. I start feeling as if I'm tromping all over something pure and white with muddy feet, defiling it. Until I arrived, this place had been perfectly silent. *I'm not welcome*, I think instinctively. My body heat is being sucked away again, into the cold water. Before long, the water's up to my chest, but I manage to get across somehow.

The massive tree stands with its roots twined around a big slab of rock.

I don't know whether the "body of the god" is the tree, the rock, or whether the shape of the two of them tangled together is what people worship. There's a little stairway in the gap between the roots and the stone, and when I go down it, I find a yawning space wide enough for about four tatami mats.

The silence here is even deeper than it was outside.

I unzip my jacket with freezing hands and take out my phone. I check to make sure it didn't get wet, then turn it on. In the darkness, every single movement sounds violently loud. With an electronic *vvum* that seems completely out of place here, the phone comes alive, and I use it as a flashlight.

This place is wholly devoid of color or warmth.

The tiny shrine the light reveals is completely gray. On a small stone altar, two four-inch urns sit side by side.

"It's the sake we carried up here."

Gently, I touch the surface. I don't know when it happened, but I'm not cold anymore.

"This is her little sister's…"

My hand closes around the urn on the left, confirming its shape. When I pick it up, there's a slight resistance and a faint, dry tearing noise. The moss had put down roots.

"And this is the one I brought."

I sit down where I am, bring the urn close to my face, and shine the light on it. The porcelain was shiny before, but now it's thickly covered with moss. It must have been a very long time. I put a thought that's been inside me all this time into words.

"…Then I was swapping with the Mitsuha from three years ago?"

I untie the braided cord sealing the lid. Underneath, there's a cork stopper.

"Were we three years out of sync? Did the swapping stop because she died three years ago when the meteorite fell?"

I pull out the cork. The faint scent of alcohol rises. I pour the sake into the lid.

"Half of her…"

I bring the light closer to it. The sake is clear, with several tiny particles floating in it. They reflect the light, glittering in the liquid.

"*Musubi*. Twisting and tangling, sometimes coming undone, then reuniting…"

I raise the lidful of sake to my lips.

"If time really can 'come undone,' then… Just one more time…"

Take me to her! I wish and down it in one gulp. When I swallow, the sound is so conspicuous it startles me. A lump of heat travels through my body. As it hits the bottom of my stomach, it bursts, scattering through me.

"……"

But nothing happens.

For a little while, I sit very still.

I'm not used to alcohol, and I feel a little warm. My head feels slightly vague and dizzy… But that's all.

It's no good. It didn't work.

I put one knee up, then stand. Abruptly, my feet tangle. My vision spins. *I'm falling*, I think.

…That's weird.

I've fallen over backward, but no matter how much time passes, my back doesn't hit the ground. My field of view rotates, slowly, up to the roof of the cave. My phone is still in my left hand. The light illuminates the ceiling.

"The comet…!"

Involuntarily, I say it out loud.

There's a drawing of an enormous comet up there.

It's a very old picture, carved into the rock: a giant traveling star, trailing its long tail across the heavens. The red and blue pigments catch the light and shimmer. Gradually, the picture begins rising away from the ceiling of the cave.

I stare.

The image, the illustrated comet, is falling toward me.

Slowly, it bears down until it's nearly on top of me. It blazes with the heat of its friction against the atmosphere, and the lump of rock fuses into glass, shining like a jewel. Even those details are clear to me.

I fall back, and my head hits the rock at the exact moment the comet strikes my body.

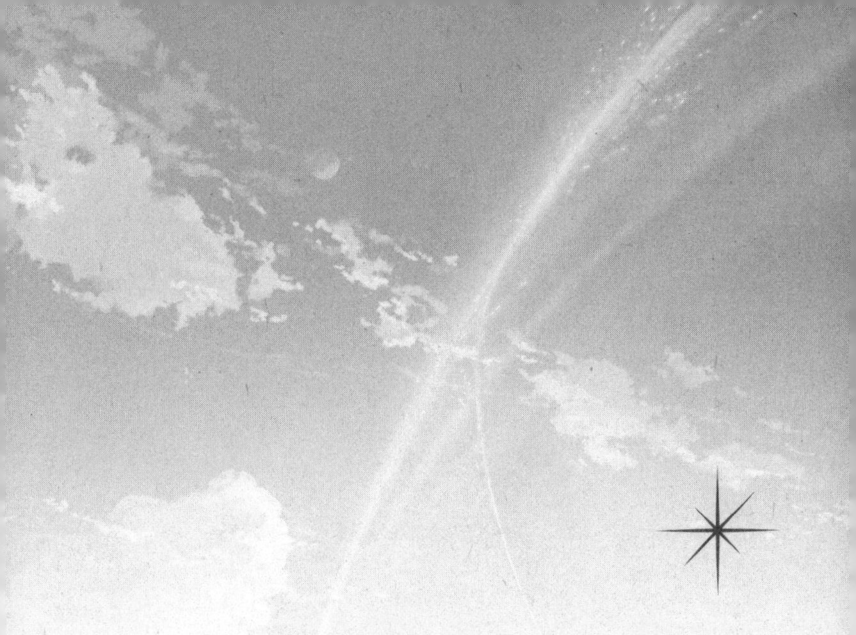

Chapter Five

Memories

Falling forever.

Or maybe rising.

In the midst of this indistinct floating sensation, the comet shines in the night sky.

Without warning, it splits, and half of it comes plummeting down.

The meteorite strikes a village in the mountains. Many people die. A lake forms, and the village is destroyed.

Time passes, and another village grows up around the lake. The lake provides fish, and the heavenly iron provides wealth. The village prospers. Ages pass, and the comet arrives again. Once again, the star falls. Once again, people die.

This has happened twice since mankind settled on these islands.

People tried to remember it. They tried to pass on the knowledge to future generations, using methods that would last longer than letters. The comet as a dragon. The comet as braided cords. The fracturing comet as the gestures of a dance.

Once again, ages pass.

I hear a baby crying.

"Your name is Mitsuha."

A mother's gentle voice.

Then, with a brutal sensation, the umbilical cord is cut.

Even though we were all two who lived as one in the beginning, even though we were all connected, so humans are severed from the cord and fall into this life.

"You're both your dad's treasures."

"You're a big sister now, sweetheart."

A young couple converses. Before long, Mitsuha's little sister is born. As if in exchange for that joy, her mother falls ill.

"When is Mommy comin' back from the hospital?"

The little sister's question is innocent, but the older sister knows their mother is never coming back. Everyone dies. It's inevitable, but it isn't easy to accept.

"They couldn't save her!"

The father grieves deeply. He has never loved anyone as much as he loved his wife, and he never will again. It's both a blessing and a curse that, as they grow, his daughters look more and more like their mother.

"Taking over the shrine won't do any—"

"What are you saying?! Why do you think we formally adopted you when you married?!"

The father and grandmother quarrel more every day.

"I loved Futaba, not Miyamizu Shrine."

"Get out!"

Both the father and the grandmother are too old to change their priorities. The father can't take it, and he leaves.

"Mitsuha, Yotsuha. From now on, you'll be with your gran all the time."

In a house that echoes with the *click* of ball-weights, the three women begin their life together.

The days are peaceful enough. Even so, the feeling that her father has abandoned her becomes an indelible stain inside Mitsuha.

These are…

…Mitsuha's memories?

As if I'm being swept along helplessly by a storm-swollen torrent, I experience Mitsuha's time.

Then come the days I already know, the swapped days.

Seen through Mitsuha's eyes, Tokyo shines like an exotic foreign country. Even though we share the same senses, it's as if we're seeing completely different worlds.

"Lucky…"

I hear Mitsuha murmur.

"I bet they're together right about now."

It's the day of my date with Okudera-senpai.

"I'm goin' to Tokyo for a bit," she tells her little sister.

Tokyo?

That night, Mitsuha opens the sliding door to her grandmother's room.

"Gran, can I ask a favor…?"

Mitsuha's long hair is chopped short. She isn't the Mitsuha I know anymore.

"They say it'll look brightest tonight."

Teshigawara and the others invite her out. *Let's go watch the comet.*

Mitsuha, don't! I scream.

From behind the mirror. In the peal of the wind chimes. As the wind that stirs her hair.

Mitsuha, no, you can't go there!

Run! Get out of town before the comet falls!

But my voice doesn't reach her. She doesn't notice me.

On the night of the festival, Mitsuha and her friends look up at the comet, now closer than the moon.

The comet suddenly splits, and its shards shine, becoming countless shooting stars. One massive fragment of rock becomes a meteor and begins to fall.

Even then, gazing at it, her only thought is, *It's beautiful.*
Mitsuha, run!

I scream at the top of my lungs.

Mitsuha, run, please *run! Mitsuha, Mitsuha, Mitsuha!*
And the star falls.

Chapter Six

Reenactment

My eyes open.

In that instant, I know for sure.

I bolt upright, looking down at my body. Slim fingers. Familiar pajamas. The swell of breasts.

"It's Mitsuha…"

The words slip out. This voice, too. This narrow throat. Her blood, her flesh, her bones, her skin. Everything about Mitsuha is warm and right here.

"…She's alive…!"

I wrap my arms around my body, hugging myself. Tears spill over. Plump teardrops fall relentlessly from Mitsuha's eyes, as though a faucet has broken. Their heat brings its own joy, and I cry harder and harder. Inside my ribs, my heart leaps. I bend my knees, pressing my cheeks against the smooth kneecaps. I curl up as small as I can, wanting to hug her entire body.

Mitsuha.

Mitsuha, Mitsuha.

It's a miracle—one that might have been denied me forever, one that slipped through every possibility to be here.

                    *   *   *

"Sis, what're you doin'?"

I raise my head at the sound of the voice. Yotsuha's standing there in the open doorway.

"Oh... Little sister...," I mutter, sobs strangling my words. Yotsuha's still alive, too. She's staring, dazed, at her older sister, who's all tear-stained and snotty and feeling herself up.

"Yotsuhaaaaa!"

I rush at her, driven by an urge to scoop her up. "Yeep!" she gasps, slamming the sliding door in my face.

"Gran! Hey, Gran!" she yells, and I hear footsteps running down the stairs. "Sis finally cracked! She's completely busted!"

Her voice echoes from downstairs as she runs wailing to her grandma.

...What a rude little girl. And after I crossed space and time to save this town!

The NHK lady is yapping cheerfully. I've just changed into my school uniform and come downstairs. It's been a while since my skirt-clad lower body felt this vulnerable, and in order to shake the sensation, I'm standing tall and tough, glaring at the TV.

"Comet Tiamat has now been visible to the naked eye for about a week. It will be closest to Earth at approximately seven forty this evening, which is when it's expected to be brightest as well. The astronomy spectacular that only comes once every twelve centuries has reached its climax, and various festivities will be held all around the..."

"Tonight! There's still time!" I mutter. I'm trembling with nerves and excitement.

"Good mornin', Mitsuha. Yotsuha went on ahead today."

I turn around, and the old lady's standing there.

"Grandma! You're looking good!" Without thinking, I run over to her. She has a teapot on a tray, probably planning to enjoy some tea in the living room.

"Huh? ...My. You're..."

She pulls down her reading glasses and takes a good look at my face. Her eyes narrow softly.

"You aren't Mitsuha, are you?"

"Wha...?" How?! I feel guilty, as if some crime I knew would never come to light has been exposed. Hang on, though. This might make things easier.

"Grandma... You knew?"

There's no particular change in the old lady's expression. As she speaks, she lowers herself into a legless chair.

"No. But watchin' you lately reminded me. When I was a girl, I had some strange dreams myself."

Hear that?! That's awesome—this oughta be a quick conversation, then. Just what I'd expect from a Japanese folktale family. I join her at the table, and the old lady fills a cup for me, too. Sipping her tea, she continues her story.

"They were very odd dreams. More than dreams, really. They were another life. I became a boy I didn't know in a town I'd never seen before."

I swallow hard. Exactly like us...

"But one day, they ended, just like that. All I remember now is that I had strange dreams. My memories of who I became in them disappeared completely."

"Disappeared..."

My heart skips a beat, as if I've been told the name of a disease I'm fated to get. She's right. For a little while, I forgot Mitsuha's name. I tried to convince myself that it was all a delusion. The old lady's wrinkled face takes on a tinge of loneliness.

"So treasure who you are now and the things you're seein'. No matter how special it is, a dream's a dream. It'll disappear for sure someday, once you wake. We all had a time like that, you know: my mother, myself, and your mother."

"That's... What if...?!"

Abruptly, it hits me. This might be a role passed down through the Miyamizu family: the ability to communicate with someone living a few years in the future to escape the disaster that strikes every twelve hundred years. A shrine maiden's role. Something the Miyamizu bloodline acquired at some point...a warning system inherited across generations.

"Maybe the Miyamizus' dreams were all for today!"

I look the old lady straight in the eye, speaking firmly. "Grandma, listen."

She raises her head. From her expression, I can't tell how she'll take what I'm about to say.

"Tonight, a meteorite will strike the town of Itomori, and everyone will die."

This time, the old lady's eyebrows knit in unmistakable doubt.

"Nobody'd believe hooey like that." That old broad says some surprisingly normal stuff.

I run down the hill to the high school, silently brooding to myself.

She believes the swapping dreams but not the meteorite strike. What sort of sense of balance does she have, anyway?

I'm really late, and there's almost nobody around. The calls of the copper pheasants echo, *piichik paachik*, and it's just another peaceful morning in town. *We'll have to do it ourselves*, I think.

"There's no way I'm letting anybody die!"

I shout it out loud, emphatically, as if hammering the resolution into my own mind. I run even faster. There's not even half a day left until that meteor comes down.

"Mitsuha, wha...? Y-your hair...!"

"Girl, that hair! What on earth?!"

The second I enter the classroom, Teshigawara and Saya stare at my (Mitsuha's) face, dumbfounded.

"Oh yeah, the hair? It was way better before, right?"

As I speak, I flip the shoulder-length bob away from the back of my neck. Come to think of it, Mitsuha lopped off most of that long hair of hers at some point, didn't she? I prefer long black hair, so I'm not a fan of this... No, that's not what's important now!

"Never mind that!"

Teshigawara's mouth is hanging open so wide, I can practically hear the sound effect for shock. Saya's examining me searchingly. I look back and forth between them.

"If nothing changes, everyone's gonna die tonight!"

The hum in the classroom stops dead. All our classmates' eyes are on me.

"H-hold it, Mitsuha. What're you sayin'?!"

Saya hastily stands up, and Teshigawara grabs my arm and pulls me. As they drag me out of the classroom, my head finally cools down a bit. I guess it's only natural that they wouldn't believe me. Maybe it's like the old lady said, and it's unreasonable to expect people to buy something like this out of the blue. I was so excited about swapping for the first time in ages that I convinced myself things would just work out somehow.

Hmm. This might be tougher than I expected.

...Or so I thought, but as far as Teshigawara was concerned, that was wasted worry.

"Mitsuha, is that for real?"

"Yes, it's for real! Tonight, Comet Tiamat is going to split and turn into a meteorite, and it's hugely likely it's gonna hit this town. I can't reveal my sources, but I got the information through a reliable channel."

"That's...a full-on emergency!"

"C'mon, Tesshi, what're you lookin' so serious for? Are you really that dumb?"

Naturally, Saya isn't having any of it.

"What's this source of yours, anyway? The CIA? NASA? What're you goin' on about? 'Reliable channels'? You pretendin' you're a spy now? Honestly, Mitsuha, what's the matter with you?!"

She couldn't be more sensible. Getting desperate, I dump all the money out of Mitsuha's wallet.

"Saya, please! I'll pay, so take this and go buy whatever you want! Then at least listen to what I've got to say!"

I'm begging, and my expression is dead serious. Startled, Saya takes a long, hard look at me.

"But you're always tight with your money... You're really goin' that far?"

Huh? She is? But she burned through my money like crazy!

Saya sighs, as if she's resigned herself. "...I guess I'll have to, then. None of this makes any sense, but fine, I'll at least listen. Tesshi, gimme the key to your bike." She sets off for the main entrance, grumbling, "This ain't enough for more than a couple cheap sweets."

Good. It looks like the amount wasn't enough, but she believes I'm serious now.

"I'm goin' to the convenience store. Tesshi, you keep a close eye on Mitsuha. She ain't quite right."

And so Teshigawara and I sneak into a room in the club building nobody uses anymore and put together an evacuation plan for the town.

The goal is to get all 188 families—about five hundred people—out of the danger zone before the meteorite falls. The first thing we think of is broadcasting an evacuation order.

After we run through the inevitable ridiculous ideas—*We'll take over the prime minister's official residence! Or the Diet Building! Or the NHK Shibuya Broadcasting Center, or at least the NHK Gifu-Takayama branch office!*—we start talking about how not everybody in town will be at home with their TVs or radios on and how even more people will be out and about because of the autumn festival tonight. Then we fall silent, thinking.

"…The disaster alert system!" Teshigawara shouts suddenly.

"Disaster alert system?"

"Hunh? Don't go tellin' me you don't know. There are speakers all over town, remember?"

"Oh… That thing that starts talking out of the blue every morning and evening? Who was born, who's having a funeral, that sort of thing?"

"Yeah. You can hear that all over town for sure, whether you're inside or out. If we send the order over that…!"

"Huh? But, uh…how? That comes from the town hall, doesn't it? Would they let us broadcast stuff if we asked?"

"Pssh. No."

"Then what do we do? Hijack Town Hall? I mean, I guess we'd have a better shot at that than at taking over NHK, but…"

"Heh-heh-heh." With a creepy smile, Teshigawara types something into his phone. Geez, this guy looks happy.

"We can do this!"

He holds out his phone to me.

Superimposed frequencies, it reads, and below is an explanation.

"Wha…? Is this for real?"

Teshigawara flares his nostrils and nods proudly.

"Uh, Tesshi… Why do you even know stuff like this?"

"Well, I always fantasize before I fall asleep, y'know? About destroyin' the town, overthrowin' the school, stuff like that. Doesn't everybody?"

"Huh…?" That weirds me out a bit. But, no—this is…

"This is awesome, Tesshi! It just might work!"

Without thinking, I throw an arm around Teshigawara's shoulders.

"H-hey, don't get too close!"

"Huh?"

Whoa. Even his ears are red.

"What's this? Tesshi, are you embarrassed?"

I look up into Teshigawara's face from below, grinning at him. Well, well, Mitsuha, you're not to be taken lightly, are you? C'mon, c'mon! I press my body against him some more. Here you go—have a freebie! We're sitting side by side on an old sofa, and Tesshi's already right by the wall, so he's got nowhere to run.

"Hey, Mitsuha, cut it out!"

Teshigawara resists, big body squirming. He's a guy, for sure… Well, so am I. Then, abruptly, Teshigawara jumps up, climbing onto the back of the sofa, and yells, "I told you, knock it off! A single girl your age—that ain't proper!"

"Ha…"

Even his buzzed scalp is red. He's sweating bullets, and his eyes look almost teary.

"Ha, ha-ha-ha! Tesshi, you're such a…!"

In spite of myself, I crack up laughing.

He's a really good guy, and I'm positive I can count on him.

I thought of him as a friend before, but I'd like to meet him and the others for real and talk to them as a guy soon. Me and Mitsuha and Teshigawara and Saya. If Tsukasa and Takagi and Okudera-senpai were there, too, I know it'd be a blast.

"Sorry, Tesshi. I was just so happy you believed me…" I'm biting back laughter, and Teshigawara's sulking. "Will you help me think up the rest of the evacuation plan?"

I smile at him. Tesshi's face is still red, but even so, he nods seriously.

Once this is over, I'll come see this guy, too, I think, feeling a little bit dazzled.

"A-a-a…a bomb?!"

Saya yells. She's eating a mini shortcake from a clear plastic wrapper.

"Technically, they're called water-gel explosives. They're kinda like dynamite," Teshigawara tells her, sounding proud. He's crunching away on potato chips, and I'm noshing on chocolate drops. Saya bought a ton of convenience-store food and spread it all over the desk, so it sort of feels like we're having a party.

Teshigawara and I are standing behind a map, outlining our carefully engineered evacuation plan to Saya. I almost want to play some energetic music to set the stage. Something percussive and a bit unhinged—something that sounds like a strategy meeting.

Taking a gulp of coffee milk from a pint-size pack, Teshigawara continues. "There's lots of explosives in my dad's company's warehouse, for construction stuff. If I don't have to worry about gettin' caught afterward, I can snatch as much as we need."

"Then, next," I say, opening a melon bread wrapper. I'm really hungry, and for some reason, everything I eat when I'm in Mitsuha's body tastes really good.

"Y-y-y...you're gonna hijack the signal?!" Saya's voice cracks.

Munching on curry bread, Teshigawara explains. "Rural wireless disaster alert systems like ours are easy to take over, as long as you know the transmission frequency and the superimposed wake-up frequency. The speakers are made so they'll activate as long as a specific frequency is layered over the audio."

Melon bread in one hand, I pick up where he left off. "That means we can send the evacuation order all over town from the school broadcasting room."

I point at the map of Itomori. There's a circle with a diameter of a little less than a mile, centered on Miyamizu Shrine, and I trace its edge with my finger.

"This is the area that's supposed to take damage from the meteorite. As you can see, Itomori High is outside it." I tap on the location of the high school.

"In other words, we just need to evacuate people here, to the schoolyard."

"B-but that's…" Saya begins stammering nervously. "That's a full-blown crime!"

Even as she says it, she's putting the strawberry—which she saved for last—in her mouth.

"We'll never get the people around here to move without committing a crime," I tell her coolly, sweeping away the chocolate drops I'd scattered over the map. That's right. As long as it gets the people inside this circle to leave, it doesn't matter whether it's a crime or not.

"Y'know, Mitsuha, it's like you're a different person."

I grin and take a big bite of melon bread. When I'm in this body, I unconsciously start talking a bit like a girl, but I've completely abandoned trying to act like Mitsuha. As long as these guys are still safe when everything's over, nothing else matters. As long as we're all alive, things will work out.

"…So. You're the one in charge of the broadcast, Saya," I tell her cheerfully.

"Why?!"

"Well, you're in the broadcasting club, right?"

"Plus, your big sis is in charge of the Town Hall broadcast. Get her to tell you the wireless frequency," says Teshigawara.

"Huh? I can't just…"

Ignoring Saya's protest, Teshigawara happily points to himself. "I'm the explosives guy!"

"And I'm going to go talk to the mayor," I say, pointing to myself.

"Huh?!" Saya is speechless, and Teshigawara picks up the explanation.

"We can probably set up the evacuation on our own with the plan we just talked about. But if the town hall and firefighters don't come out at the end, there's no way we'll get everybody in all one hundred eighty-eight families to move, y'know?"

"That's why we need to persuade the mayor," I tell her. "I'm his daughter. If I can explain it to him rationally, I'm sure he'll understand."

Teshigawara folds his arms and nods, patting himself on the back. "It's a perfect strategy!" That's exactly how I feel. True, our methods are a bit rough, but I don't think there's any other way to do it.

"Haaaaaah…" Saya watches us with her mouth agape, though I can't tell whether she's amazed or appalled. "Well, I'm impressed you thought it through that far, but… This is all just in case something happens, isn't it?"

"Huh?"

I hadn't expected that question this late in the game, and I'm at a loss for words.

"Uh…not exactly…"

If Saya doesn't get on board, this plan won't work. I don't know what to tell her, and I search for something to say.

"That ain't necessarily so!" Abruptly, Teshigawara jumps in, thrusting out the screen on his phone. "Do you know how Itomori Lake got made?"

Saya and I squint at the screen. It's a site that looks like the town's home page, with a header that says *The Origins of Itomori Lake*. Then the words *A meteoric lake from twelve hundred years ago*, and *Incredibly rare for Japan*.

"It's a meteoric lake! This place already had at least one meteorite strike!"

As Teshigawara says this, a triumphant look on his face, something clicks in my mind. I start speaking before I even know what it is. "That's right—he's right… That's why!"

That's why there was a picture of the comet in a place like that, I realize. Comet Tiamat has a twelve-hundred-year cycle. Itomori Lake is a twelve-hundred-year-old meteoric lake. The meteorite strikes every twelve hundred years, when the comet passes. A presaged disaster. That means it should be avoidable. That picture was both a message and a warning.

I feel as if I've picked up an unexpected ally. I can't hold still any longer. The preparations for this were laid a thousand years ago!

"Good one, Tesshi!"

Without thinking, I stick out my fist, and Teshigawara bumps it. "Yeah!"

This will work. It's gonna work!

"Let's do this!"

We turn to Saya, speaking in unison, spit flying with enthusiasm.

"…What are you talking about?"

The voice is rough and heavy, like the sound of scissors cutting into thick cardboard.

I get increasingly flustered. I talk louder, so as not to get steam-rolled. "I told you! You have to evacuate the townspeople, just in case, or—"

"Be quiet a minute."

His voice isn't raised at all, but it shuts me up.

Mitsuha's dad, Mayor Miyamizu, closes his eyes wearily and leans back in the upholstered chair in his office. The thick leather creaks audibly. Then he exhales, slowly, and gazes out the window. The shadows of the leaves sway in the bright afternoon sunlight.

"…The comet is going to split in two and fall on this town? More than five hundred people could die?"

He taps the desk with his fingertips, leaving a long pause. Then finally, he returns his gaze to me. The backs of my knees are sweating. For the first time, I realize that's where Mitsuha gets sweaty when she's nervous.

"I know it's hard to believe, but I do have grounds for—"

"How dare you come to me with nonsense like that!"

Out of nowhere, he explodes. The creases between his eyes grow deeper. "Do delusions run in the Miyamizu bloodline?" he grumbles quietly, as if talking to himself. He fixes me with a piercing look and speaks in a low tone. "Listen, Mitsuha. If you're being serious with me, then you are ill."

"…Wha—?"

The words won't come. I realize the confidence I'd had in the clubroom just thirty minutes ago is gone without a trace. The uneasy feeling that I'm actually misguided is building rapidly. No, that's not true. I'm not deluded, and I'm not sick. I'm—

"I'll send a car around for you." The mayor picks up the phone, suddenly sounding concerned. He starts dialing, initiating a call even as he's speaking to me. "Have a doctor at the city hospital look at you. After that, I'll hear what you have to say."

The words send an unpleasant jolt through me. This guy is seriously treating me, his own daughter, like a head case. The second it registers, my whole body goes as cold as ice, while the core of my brain flares so hot it might as well be on fire.

It's rage.

"—Don't you talk down to me, you bastard!"

The words come out as a scream. The mayor's wide eyes are right in front of me. Without thinking, I've grabbed him by his necktie and hauled him up. The phone receiver falls to the floor beside the desk, and I hear the tiny buzz of a dead line.

"…Ah—"

I relax my grip. Slowly, the man's face recedes. Mayor Miyamizu's lips are slack and trembling slightly, in either shock or bewilderment. We're staring each other in the eye. Neither of us is able to look away. A cold sweat opens every pore on my body.

"Mitsuha."

The mayor sounds as if he's struggling to squeeze the air out.

"No… Who are you?"

He's trembling. With a nasty sensation, like a little winged bug the wind carried in, the words linger in my ears for a very long time.

Faintly, I can hear the reverberations of hammering in the distance. It's sometime between midday and evening. The town is too quiet, and even sounds from very far off reach my ears on the breeze. *Tok-tok, tok-tok.*

After leaving the mayor's office, I trudge along the hill road overlooking the lake, picturing a nail being driven into hard lumber in time with the noise. An iron nail, wedged into dark, cramped splinters, destined to rust. *They're probably getting ready for the autumn festival up at the shrine*, I think absently, gazing at the wooden lanterns that line the road.

Hearing children's voices above me—"'Kay, see you later!"—I look up.

Farther up the slope, kids with backpacks are waving to one another.

"Mm-hmm, I'll see you at the festival."

"Meet us below the shrine."

With that, a boy and girl part ways with their friend and come running toward me. They're in the middle years of elementary school, probably about Yotsuha's age.

It fell on the shrine.

"Don't go!" The boy's just about to run past me, and without thinking, I grab his shoulders. "Get out of town! Tell your friends, too!"

Between my arms, the expression of a kid I don't even know slides into terror.

"Wh-what's wrong with you?!"

He shoves my hands away. I come back to my senses.

"Sis!"

When I turn toward the voice, Yotsuha's running down the hill toward me, wearing her backpack and a worried expression. The two kids make a break for it and dash away. I can't do stuff like this. I'll just seem creepy.

"Sis?! What'd you do to those kids?!" Yotsuha pounces on me, grabbing my arms and looking up into my face.

What am I supposed to do now?

I look at Yotsuha. She's anxiously waiting for me to say something. "If Mitsuha had tried..." I murmur the thoughts as they come. "Could she have talked him into it? Is it just me who can't do it?" Yotsuha's bewildered, but I ignore her and keep going. "Yotsuha, before evening comes, take Grandma and get out of town."

"Huh?"

"If you stay here, you'll die!"

"What?! Sis, c'mon—what're you talkin' about?!"

"This is important," I tell her, but Yotsuha desperately raises her voice, trying to push my words back at me.

"Sis, snap out of it!"

Her eyes are tearing up. She's scared. As Yotsuha speaks, she stands on her tiptoes, gazing into my eyes. "You took off for Tokyo all of a sudden yesterday, too. You've been weird all the time lately, Sis!"

"Huh?"

I feel a strange sense of wrongness... Tokyo?

"Yotsuha, did you just say Tokyo?"

"Heeey, Mitsuhaaa!"

It's Saya. When I look up, she's waving wildly from the back of the bike Teshigawara's pedaling. It brakes, skidding a bit on the asphalt.

"Did you talk to your dad?! How'd it go?!"

Teshigawara's leaning forward. I can't respond. I'm confused. I don't know what to think anymore. The mayor wouldn't listen to a word I said. Not only that, the guy asked his own daughter who she was. *I* made him do that. Is it because I'm in Mitsuha? Is that why it didn't work? In that case, where is she now? Yotsuha says Mitsuha went to Tokyo yesterday. Why? When was "yesterday"?

"Hey, Mitsuha?" I hear Teshigawara's puzzled voice.

"What's wrong with your sis?" Sayaka asks Yotsuha.

Where is Mitsuha? Where am I, right now?

What if...?

I lift my eyes. Beyond the houses, the rolling outlines of mountains build on each other, and beyond them, there's a misty blue ridgeline. The mountain I climbed. The body of the god at the peak. The place where I drank the sake. A light, cold wind blows up from the lake, stirring Mitsuha's newly short hair. The strands stroke my cheeks softly, almost like someone's fingertips.

"Is she...there?" I mutter.

"Huh? What? What's the matter? Is somethin' up there?"

Yotsuha and Saya and Teshigawara all follow my gaze. Mitsuha, if you're there—

"Tesshi, let me borrow your bike!"

Even as I speak, I grab the handlebars, wrenching it away from him. I straddle the seat, then kick off.

"Hey, wha—? Mitsuha!"

The seat's really high. Standing up to pedal, I start climbing the hill road.

"Mitsuha, what about the operation?!"

As I get farther away, Teshigawara yells after me. He sounds like he might be about to cry.

"Get ready, just like we planned! Please!"

My shout echoes through the hushed town. Severed from her body, Mitsuha's voice rebounds between the mountains and the lake, filling the air for a moment. As if chasing that voice, I stomp on the pedals with all my might.

✳   ✳   ✳

Someone's tapping my cheek.

It's a very faint pressure, probably just the tip of a middle finger.

Whoever it is, is being gentle, trying not to hurt me. The fingertip is very cold. Chilly, as if a moment earlier it had been touching ice. Who in the world would wake me up like that?

I open my eyes.

Huh?

It's really dark. Maybe it's still night.

Another tap on my cheek. No… This is water. Drops of water have been hitting my face. When I sit up, I finally notice.

"…I'm Taki!" Without meaning to, I say it out loud.

As I climb the narrow stone steps, the evening sun lances straight into my eyes.

I must have been in the dark for quite a while. Taki's eyes sting and tear up. When I've climbed all the way to the top, my guess is confirmed: I'm on the mountain of the body of the god.

What is Taki doing here?

Without really understanding what's going on, I emerge from beneath the giant tree and begin walking across the basin. Taki is wearing a heavy camping parka and hiking shoes with thick rubber soles. The ground is soft and wet, and it might have just stopped raining—the low grass is thick with water droplets. When I look up, though, the sky is perfectly clear. Thin, shredded clouds stream in the wind, glowing and golden.

My memories are oddly vague.

Still unable to remember anything, before long I come to the edge of the basin, the foot of the slope. I look up the hill. This whole area is a depression. The top of this slope is the top of the mountain. I start climbing. As I do, I search my memories, trying to remember what I was doing before I came here. Then my fingers touch the edge.

Festival music. A light summer kimono. My own face, hair cut short, reflected in a mirror.

That's right.

Yesterday was the autumn festival. Tesshi and Saya asked me to go, so I put on my traditional clothes and went out. It was the day the comet was supposed to be brightest, so we were going to watch. Yes, that was it. It all seems very distant somehow, but it was definitely yesterday.

My new haircut really startled Tesshi and Saya. Tesshi's mouth gaped so wide, you could practically hear the sound effect for shock. They were so shaken I felt a little sorry for them. The entire walk to the hill, they whispered behind my back.

"Hey, do you think she got her heart broken?"

"Why do you go there?! Are you some old guy from last century?"

When we'd climbed all the way up the narrow one-lane road and turned at the traffic mirror, there it was: an enormous comet in the night sky, straight above us. Its long, streaming tail shone emerald green, and its head was brighter than the moon. If I strained my eyes, I could see particles glittering around it like fine dust. We forgot to talk to each other and just stood there with our mouths open like idiots, staring, fascinated, for a long time.

Then, at some point, I realized the comet had split. There were two big, bright tips, and one seemed to be steadily coming closer. Before long, several delicate shooting stars began shining around it. It was like the heavens were falling. No—that night, the stars actually did fall. It was a sight straight out of a dream, an impossibly beautiful night sky.

I finally reach the top of the slope. The wind buffeting me is cold. Below me, a blanket of clouds unfolds like a shining carpet. Through them, I can see Itomori Lake, which is beginning to be tinted with faint blue shadows.

Huh? I think.

How strange.

For the past little while, I've been shaking so hard it's as if someone's put me on ice.

Out of nowhere, I'm so scared I can't handle it.

I'm terrified, anxious, sad, and lonely, and it feels like I might lose my mind. I'm gushing cold sweat as though a tap has broken.

What if...?

Maybe I have gone crazy. Maybe I cracked before I even knew it was happening.

I'm scared. I'm scared. I want to scream right this minute, but sticky breath is the only thing that comes out of my throat. My eyelids open wider and wider, driven by a will that isn't mine. The surfaces of my eyes are desert dry. They're gazing at the lake. I know. I've seen it.

Itomori is gone.

A bigger round lake has formed, overlapping Itomori Lake.

Somewhere inside my mind, I think, *Well, of course it has*.

After a thing like that fell on us.

After that leaden, sweltering mass came down on our heads.

That's right.

That night, I...

It's as if my joints have broken without a sound. I drop to my knees on the spot.

That night...I...

The air that leaks from my throat becomes a voice, just barely.

"That night..."

Taki's memories flood into me. The comet disaster that destroyed an entire town. The fact that Taki really lived in Tokyo three years in the future. The fact that, by then, I wasn't anywhere anymore. The night the star fell. Back then, I...

"...I died...?"

✳ ✳ ✳

Where do human memories live?

Are they in the synaptic circuitry of the brain? Do retinas and fingertips hold memories, too? Or is there an invisible, amorphous, mistlike, spiritual collective somewhere, and that's where the memories reside? Something we'd call the heart or the mind or the soul. Is it something you can take out and stick back in, like a memory card with an OS on it?

The asphalt cut out a while back, and I've been pedaling over unpaved mountain roads. The low sun flickers through the gaps among the trees. Mitsuha's body is sweating nonstop, and my bangs are plastered to my forehead. As I pedal, I wipe the hair out of my face along with the sweat.

Mitsuha's soul must be in my body right now. After all, my heart's here, in hers. But… This is something I've been thinking for a while.

Even now, we're together.

Mitsuha, or at least some fragment of her heart, is still here. For example, her fingers remember the shape of her uniform. When I put it on, I naturally know the length of the zipper and the stiffness of the collar. When Mitsuha's eyes see her friends, I feel relieved and happy. Without even asking, I can tell who Mitsuha likes and who she's not comfortable around. When I see her grandma, memories I shouldn't even have rise hazily in my mind, like a projector with broken focus. Body and memories and emotions are bound together inseparably.

Taki.

I've been hearing Mitsuha's voice inside this body for a while now.

Taki, Taki.

Her tone is earnest, pleading, as if she's about to cry. A voice trembling with loneliness, like the glimmer of distant stars.

The blurry image sharpens. *Taki*, Mitsuha's calling.

"Don't you remember me?"

And then I recall her memories of that day.

✳ ✳ ✳

That day, instead of going to school, Mitsuha got on a train.

She went to a big terminal station, where the Shinkansen to Tokyo stopped. The local train she took to get there was empty, despite the fact that it was rush hour, when students were heading to school. Since there were no schools along the track, everyone who commuted around here drove.

"I'm goin' into Tokyo for a bit."

This had been Mitsuha's abrupt announcement to her little sister when they left the house that morning.

"Huh? Now? Why?!" Yotsuha asks, startled.

"Um… For a date?"

"Wha—?! Sis, you have a boyfriend in Tokyo?!"

"Uh, well… It's not my date." Unsure how to explain herself, Mitsuha breaks into a run. "I'll be back tonight. Don't worry!"

Gazing at the scenery flying past the window of the bullet train, Mitsuha wonders:

Why am I crashin' Okudera-senpai and Taki's date? It's not like the three of us can just hang out together. Besides, I've never been to Tokyo before. Will I even be able to find Taki? Even if I do, will it bother him that I'm showin' up out of the blue? Will he be surprised? Maybe he'll be upset…

With an uncomplicated ease almost inviting disappointment, the Shinkansen slides into Tokyo. The incredible crowds leave Mitsuha breathless, but she tries calling my cell. *"…Because the unit is out of range or turned off, the number you are trying to reach is…"* She hangs up. Just like the other calls, it didn't go through.

I'll never find him, Mitsuha thinks.

Still, after staring at the station information board like it's a quiz, she heads into the city, relying on her vague memories.

But if I do see him…

She rides the Yamanote Line, the city bus, walks, takes another train, then walks some more.

What'll I do? It probably will bother him, right? Maybe it'll be awkward. Or maybe—

She sees the words *Comet Tiamat at Closest Point Tomorrow* on a big outdoor TV screen.

Or, if I do find him, just maybe, will he—?

Tired from walking, she gazes at the sparkling lights of the buildings from a pedestrian bridge and thinks, almost praying:

If I find Taki, maybe he'll be just a little bit happy…

She starts walking again, still thinking.

I'll never find him searchin' randomly like this. I won't, but I know one thing for sure. If we meet, we'll know right away. "You're the one who was in me. I'm the one who was in you."

Mitsuha's certain of this, as if it's as simple as two plus two.

The evening sun sinks through the gap between the station platform roofs, as weak as a dying flashlight.

Mitsuha's feet are sore from all the walking she's done, and she plants herself on a bench with her legs kicked out in front of her. She stares absently at the setting sun, which is much paler and less reliable than in Itomori.

A musical chime plays, and a voice announces: *"The local train to…Chiba…is arriving on…Track Four."* A yellow train glides onto the platform. The cars kick up a warm wind that ruffles her hair. Mitsuha gazes at the train windows without really seeing them.

Abruptly, her breath catches.

She jumps to her feet as if she's been stung.

He'd been there, in the window that had just passed in front of her.

Mitsuha breaks into a sprint. The cars have stopped, and she catches up to the window almost immediately. The evening train is crowded, though, and she can't find him again from outside. With a sound like a giant exhalation, the doors open. The car's so tightly packed that the people are practically spilling out, making Mitsuha shiver. Even so—murmuring "Excuse me" and sweating behind the knees—she pushes her way into the crowd. With another giant sigh, the doors close. The train begins moving. Repeating "Excuse me" over and over, little by little, Mitsuha works her way forward. Then, in front of one boy, she stops. The sounds around her vanish.

It's me. The middle school "me" from three years ago.

✳　✳　✳

I can't go any higher on the bike.

No sooner have I had the thought than the front wheel catches on a root, and I slip.

On reflex, I grab the trunk of a nearby tree. The bike slips out from under me and tumbles down the slope, hitting the ground about ten feet below with a huge racket. The wheels are bent all out of shape. "Sorry, Teshigawara," I mutter softly, and I take off running up the narrow mountain track.

Why did I forget? Why didn't I remember until just now?

As I run, I stare at the memories welling up inside me.

Mitsuha, that day, three years ago, you came to see me—

✳　✳　✳

Taki. Taki, Taki.

For a while now, Mitsuha has been silently rolling my name around on her tongue. I haven't noticed her at all, even though I'm right in front of her. She keeps fretting over what tone she should use to address me and what expression she should wear, so earnestly she seems liable to burst into tears. Then, forcing a bright smile, she says:

"Taki."

The middle school me is startled hearing my name out of the blue, and I glance up. We're still about the same height, so her big, vaguely teary eyes are right in front of me.

"Huh…?"

"Um, do you…"

Smiling desperately, Mitsuha points to herself. I'm bewildered.

"…Huh?"

"Don't you remember me?" asks this stranger, timidly, looking at me through her lashes.

"Who're you?"

Mitsuha gives a small, breathy shriek, then quickly turns red. She lowers her eyes, speaking in a voice that's barely audible.

"Oh… I'm sorry…"

The train sways. The passengers all adjust to keep their balance, except for Mitsuha, who staggers into me. Her hair brushes the tip of my nose, and I catch the faint scent of shampoo. "I'm sorry," she mumbles again.

Weird girl, thinks middle school me.

Mitsuha's muddled mind races desperately. But you're Taki, so why…? For both of us, time passes awkwardly.

"The next station is… Yotsuya." The announcement offers Mitsuha a bit of relief. At the same time, though, she feels unbearably sad. Still, she can't stay here any longer. The doors open, and she moves with the rest of the crowd to exit the train.

Watching her receding back, I suddenly think, *Maybe this weird girl is somebody I should know.* This inexplicable, intense impulse drives me to call out.

"'Scuse me! What's your name?"

Mitsuha turns back, but the waves of disembarking passengers push her farther away. Hurriedly, she undoes the braided cord tying back her hair. She holds it out to me and shouts:

"Mitsuha!"

Without thinking, I reach for it. It's a vivid orange, like a thin

ray of evening sun in the dim train. I shove my way into the crowd
and grab that color tight.

"My name is Mitsuha!"

✳   ✳   ✳

That day, three years ago, you came to see me.

Finally, I know.

A girl I didn't recognize spoke to me on the train once. To me,
that was all it'd been, and I completely forgot about it. But Mitsuha
had come to Tokyo carrying the weight of all those feelings, had
been hurt badly, gone back to her own town, and cut her hair.

There's a lump in my throat. Still, there's nothing I can do about
it now, so I just keep running, hell for leather. My (Mitsuha's) face
and body are smeared with sweat and dirt. The next thing I know,
the trees have ended, and I'm in a rocky, mossy area, with clouds like
a golden carpet below me.

I've finally reached the peak.

I suck in a huge chestful of cold air. Then, as if I'm expelling
all my emotions from the pit of my stomach, I yell at the top of my
lungs.

"Mitsuhaaaa!"

I hear a voice.

I lift my head. I stand, looking around.

I'm up on the rocky area surrounding the body of the god's
basin. The evening sun is almost gone, and all the shadows are
stretched and elongated. The world is divided sharply into light and
darkness, but there's no one around.

"...Taki?" I murmur.

I draw in a deep breath of cold air. Then I shout, using Taki's
throat:

"Takiiii!"

*   *   *

I hear it.

She's here. Mitsuha is here.

I set off running, climbing the slope up to the mountain's peak.

I do a complete 360 scan of the area, but no one's there... She has to be here, though. I feel it in my core.

"Mitsuhaaa! You're here, aren't you? In my body!"

It's Taki!

I'm sure of it. I shout a question into the empty sky:

"Taki! Taki, where are you?! I can hear you, but I can't—!"

I start sprinting around the rim of the basin.

I can hear a voice. Just a voice.

I don't really know whether it—my voice, Mitsuha's voice—is actually creating sound or whether it's just echoing in something like my soul. After all, even if we're in the same place, we must still be three years apart.

"Mitsuha, where are you?!"

Even so, I shout. I can't *not* shout. I sprint around the edge of the basin with everything I've got. If I do—

If I do, I'll catch up to Taki. I run, spurred on by that delusion.

"Oh!"

Crying out in spite of myself, I stop.

I stop, hastily looking back.

Just now, I'm positive I passed her.

There's a warm presence in front of me. My heart is leaping in my chest.

I can't see him, but I know Taki's here, very close to me.

My heart is racing.

He's here. I reach out my hand.

She's here. I reach out my hand.

…But my fingers touch nothing.

"Mitsuha?"

I wait for a response. Nobody answers.

It's no good, then? We can't meet? One more time, I look around. I'm standing stock-still, up on the mountain, all alone.

At my wits' end, I lower my head and let out a long, thin breath.

The wind blows gently, softly lifting my hair. My sweat has dried completely. Sensing a sudden drop in the temperature, I glance at the evening sun. While I was distracted, it slipped below the clouds. Released from direct sunlight, light and shadow melt together, and the world's outlines grow soft and vague. The sky is still bright, but the Earth is enveloped in pale shadows. The air is filled with pink, indirect light.

That's right. There were names for this time of day. Twilight, *tasogare*. The time when the outlines blur, when you might encounter something not of this world. I murmur its old name.

Half-light.

Our voices overlap.

It can't be.

Slowly, I shift my gaze away from the clouds to the space right in front of me.

Mitsuha's there.

She's watching me, eyes wide and round, mouth hanging open.

That lame expression strikes me as funny and lovable. The emotion is stronger than my surprise, and, slowly, I start to smile.

"Mitsuha."

When I call to her, Mitsuha's eyes rapidly fill with tears.

"…Taki? Taki? Taki? Taki?"

As she repeats herself like an idiot, her hands find my arms. Her fingers tighten, squeezing.

"Taki, you're here for real!"

Her voice sounds hoarse and tight. Big tears roll down her cheeks.

We've finally met. Really met. We're facing each other, Mitsuha as Mitsuha, me as myself, in our own bodies. I feel deeply relieved. A sense of profound peace wells up inside me, as if, after being abroad for a long time in a country where I didn't know the language, I've finally come home. A calm joy fills me.

Mitsuha just keeps sobbing.

"I came to see you," I tell her.

Her tears are as clear and round as little marbles.

I smile and keep going. "Seriously, it was a rough trip! You're way out here."

That's right: way, way out here. Somewhere even the time is different.

Mitsuha looks at me, blinking.

"Huh? But... How? Back then, I..."

"I drank the sake you made."

As I tell her, remembering how much I've gone through for this, Mitsuha's tears stop dead.

"Huh...?"

She's speechless. Well, sure she is. Anybody would be really moved by that, right?

"Y...y..."

Slowly, Mitsuha backs away from me... Hmm?

"Y...you drank that?!"

"Huh?"

"Idiot! Pervert!"

"Huh—? Wha...?!"

Her face is bright red. Apparently, she's mad. Wait, is that something to get mad about?!

"Oh, and—! You touched my chest, didn't you?!"

"What?!" I'm completely rattled. "H-how do you know about…?"

"Yotsuha saw you!" Mitsuha plants her hands on her hips, talking as though she's scolding a child.

"Uh, yeah, sorry… I just…" Tch! Rotten little blabbermouth. My palms are getting sweaty. An excuse. I've gotta give her an excuse. On the spur of the moment, I blurt out, "Once! It was just once!"

Like that's any kind of excuse! I'm a moron!

"…Just once? Hmm…"

Huh? She's considering it. So "just once" is okay? I might actually get through this. However, as if correcting herself, Mitsuha's eyebrows come down.

"No, it's the same no matter how many times you do it! Idiot!"

So it's not going to work. Giving up, I clap my hands together and duck my head in apology. "Sorry!" I really can't tell her that I actually felt 'em up every time.

"Oh, that's…"

Mitsuha's expression changes abruptly. She points at my right hand in surprise. I glance at my wrist.

"Oh, yeah. This."

It's the braided cord. The one she gave me three years ago. I undo the little metal fastener that keeps it in place and unwind it from my wrist, talking to Mitsuha as I work.

"Listen, don't come visit me before we meet. How was I supposed to know it was you?" I hand the cord to Mitsuha. "Here." Remembering what she felt on that train, a softness fills my chest. "I've had it for three years. This time, you hang on to it."

Mitsuha looks up from the cord in her hands and smiles happily. "Uh-huh!" When she smiles— I hadn't noticed before, but it's like the whole world is happy right along with her.

Mitsuha wraps the cord around her head vertically, like a headband, and ties it into a bow over her left ear.

"How's this?" She blushes, looking up at me through her lashes. The braided cord bounces at the side of her bob, like a ribbon.

"Uh…"

It doesn't really work, I think. It's sort of little-kiddish. And she didn't have to chop off that much hair. First she shows up without asking, then she gets traumatized for no reason… I like long black hair, all right?

That's my immediate reaction. In cases like this, though, compliments are the best move. Even I know that. Even the **Conversation skills for the person who's never, ever been the tiniest bit popular!** link Mitsuha sent me said it was always safe to compliment women.

"…Well, it's not bad."

"Wha—?!" Mitsuha's expression immediately clouds over. Huh? "You don't think it looks good on me!"

"Huh?!" How'd she know?!

"Ha…ha-ha… Sorry."

"Honestly! You're such a…!"

She turns her face away, thoroughly disgusted. What is this? Talking to girls is friggin' impossible…

Then Mitsuha bursts out laughing. She holds her sides, giggling. What's with her, anyway? Crying and getting mad and laughing… Still, watching her, the urge starts building inside me, too. I look down, put a hand over my face, and chuckle. Mitsuha's cracking up right along with me. For some reason, we've started enjoying ourselves. We laugh out loud together. In our corner of the softly shining, half-lit world, we giggle and titter like little kids.

Bit by bit, the temperature is falling. Little by little, the light is fading.

"Mitsuha."

I suddenly remember the way I felt when I was a kid, when I'd played my heart out after school, wanting to stay with my friends for hours and hours longer but knowing it was almost time to go home.

"You've still got things you need to do. Listen."

I outline the plan for her that I'd hatched with Teshigawara and Saya. As she listens, Mitsuha nods seriously, and I realize she remembers that the star fell, that the town vanished. That she died once. For her, tonight is a reenactment.

"It's here..."

Mitsuha looks up at the sky, and as she whispers, her voice trembles slightly. I follow her gaze. In the western sky, which is turning a deep, dark blue, the shape of long-tailed Comet Tiamat is faintly visible.

"It's all right. You'll make it." I say this definitively, as much to convince myself as anything.

"Yes, I'll try... Oh, half-light's already—"

Before I know it, Mitsuha's turned the color of pale shadows, too.

"—It's already over," I finish. The last traces of the evening sun are fading from the sky. Night will be here soon. As if to shove down the anxiety suddenly amassing inside me, I force a smile and speak cheerfully. "Hey, Mitsuha. So we don't forget each other after we wake up..." I take a felt-tip pen from my pocket. I catch Mitsuha's right hand, then write on her palm. "Let's write down our names. Here."

I give the pen to Mitsuha.

"...Sure!"

She breaks into a smile. It's like watching a flower bloom. She takes my right hand and sets the tip of the pen against it.

Tunk.

There's a tiny, hard noise by my feet. I look down, and there's the pen on the ground.

"Huh?" I raise my head.

There's nobody in front of me.

"What...?"

I turn this way and that.

"Mitsuha? Hey, Mitsuha?"

I call louder. No response. Unnerved, I pace the area. The shadows are sinking into blue-black darkness. Below me are leaden, featureless clouds, and in the gloom below them, I can just make out gourd-shaped Itomori Lake.

Mitsuha's gone.

Night is here.

I'm back in my own body, three years in the future.

I look at my right hand. There's no braided cord on my wrist now. On my palm, there's just one thin, short, half-drawn line. I touch it gently.

"...I was going to tell you...," I mutter quietly to the line. "No matter where in the world you are, I'll find you again. I swear."

Up in the sky, the comet's nowhere to be seen, and a few stars are beginning to twinkle.

"Your name is Mitsuha."

I close my eyes, making sure of my memories, turning them into something I can count on.

"It's okay. I remember!"

Confidence deepening, I open my eyes again. There's a white half-moon in the distant horizon.

"Mitsuha, Mitsuha... Mitsuha, Misua, Misua. Your name is Misua!"

I'm yelling her name at the half-moon.

"Your name is...!"

Abruptly, the outline of the word I meant to utter blurs.

I quickly snatch up the pen and write the first letter of her name on my palm... Or I try to.

"......!"

After a single line, my hand stops. The tip of the pen starts to tremble. I want to make it stop shaking and grip it tight. I try stabbing it in like a needle, to carve a name that won't disappear. The pen won't budge a fraction of an inch. My lips move.

"...Who are you?"

The pen falls from my hand.

They're vanishing. Your name. Your memories.

"Why did I come here?"

I want to tether them to me somehow, to scrape the fragments of memory together, so I say them aloud.

"Her... I came to see her! I came to save her! I wanted her to live!"

It's disappearing. Something so precious to me is disappearing.

"Who are you? Who are you, who are you, who are you...?"

Slipping away. Even the emotions I know I felt are leaving me.

"Somebody important, somebody I can't forget, somebody I didn't want to forget!"

Everything's vanishing, sorrow and love alike. I don't even know why I'm crying now. My emotions are disintegrating, crumbling like a sand castle.

"Who are you, who are you, who...?"

After the sand has completely eroded, just one thing remains. I know it's loneliness. In that moment, I understand. From now on, this feeling will be all that stays with me. I'll hold nothing but loneliness, a burden someone's forced me to take.

Fine, I think defiantly. Even if the world is cruel, even if all I have is loneliness, I'll still live with everything I've got. Even if this emotion is all I have, I'll keep struggling. Even if we're separated, even if we never meet again, I'll fight. As if I'd ever resign myself to this! The powerful, fleeting resolution feels as though I'm picking a fight with the gods. Very soon, I'll forget even the fact that I've forgotten something.

And so, making that single emotion my foothold, I demand of the night sky one last time:

"What's your name?"

The cry becomes an echo, rebounding off the dark mountains. Asking its question of the void over and over, it diminishes, bit by bit.

Finally, silence descends.

Chapter Seven

Struggle, Magnificently

I run.

I'm sprinting down a dark deer track, repeating his name again and again.

Taki, Taki, Taki.

It's all right. I remember. I'll never forget.

At last, through the gaps in the trees, I begin catching glimpses of the lights of Itomori. The wind carries faint, scattered snatches of festival music to me.

Taki, Taki, Taki.

When I look up at the sky, Comet Tiamat is there, shining brighter than the moon, its long tail trailing behind it. The terror nearly makes me recoil, but I scream his name and stomp it down.

Your name is Taki!

I hear the sound of a moped, and when I raise my head, a headlight comes up over the slope and shines right in my eyes.

"Tesshi!" I shout, running up to it.

"Mitsuha! Where the heck you been?!"

He sounds like he's scolding me, but I really can't explain. Tesshi's in his school uniform with the sleeves rolled up, and he's wearing a helmet with a big light attached to it, like he's going spe-lunking. I give him Taki's message.

"He said he broke your bike, and he's sorry."

"Huh? Who did?"

"I did!"

Tesshi's eyebrows furrow, but he shuts off the moped's engine and turns on his helmet light without a word. He breaks into a run. "You better gimme the whole story later!" he says in a loud, rough voice.

ITOMORI SUBSTATION—COMPANY-OWNED LAND: KEEP OUT, says the plate on the chain-link fence. Beyond it, transformers and steel towers form a complicated silhouette. It's an unmanned facility, and the only lights I can see are the red lamps on machinery here and there.

"That thing's comin' down? For real?!" Tesshi asks, looking up at the sky.

We're in front of the substation's chain-link fence, gazing at the glittering comet.

"It will! I saw it happen!"

As I speak, I look him straight in the eye. We've got two hours until it falls. There's no time to explain.

For a moment, Tesshi looks dubious. Then, with a sharp "Hah!" he grins. His smile looks like something he's mustered out of sheer desperation. "You saw it, huh?! Then I guess we've gotta do this!"

Tesshi practically rips opens his sports bag. It's stuffed with tubes that look like race batons wrapped in brown paper: water-gel explosives. I gulp. Tesshi takes out a big bolt cutter, sets its blades against the chain wrapped around the substation gate, and says, "Mitsuha. If we do this, there's no goin' back."

"Please. I'll take all the responsibility."

"Moron! That ain't what I'm askin'!" Tesshi sounds angry, and for some reason, he's blushing a bit. "Well, we're both criminals now!"

He cuts the chain, and the loud rattle shatters the darkness.

"When the power in town goes out, the school should switch over to the emergency generator right away! You'll be able to use the broadcastin' equipment then!"

Tesshi shouts in the direction of the smartphone. He's driving the moped, and I'm behind him, holding the phone up to his mouth. Almost no cars pass us, and we're starting to see the lights of scattered houses along the dark prefectural road. We're heading for an area between the slopes of the mountains, where the lights are concentrated: Miyamizu Shrine, the site of the autumn festival. Out of nowhere, I feel an odd nostalgia, as if I've come back home after a long time away.

"Mitsuha, she wants to talk to you."

"Hello? Saya?!" I put the smartphone to my own ear.

"Waaaaaah, Mitsuhaaaa!" Saya sounds like she's in tears. "C'mon, do I really have to do this?!"

Her anxious voice sends a pang through my heart. If I were in her shoes, I'd probably be crying, too. Even sneaking by yourself into the broadcasting room at night is something you'd do only for a friend.

"Saya, I'm sorry, but I'm beggin' you! Please!" At this point, that's all I can say. "I'll never ask you for anythin' else as long as I live, but if we don't do this, a lot of people are gonna die! Once you start the announcement, repeat it for as long as you can!"

There's no response. All I can hear from the receiver are little muffled sniffling noises.

"Saya? Saya!"

I start getting nervous.

Abruptly, I hear a tiny voice. "Okay! Agh, I don't even care anymore! You tell Tesshi he better buy me somethin', too!"

"What'd she say?"

Putting the smartphone in my skirt pocket, I yell back loud enough to be heard over the moped's engine. "That you better buy her somethin', too!"

"Awright, let's do this!"

Tesshi shouts determinedly, as if trying to suppress something, and just then, behind us, there's a bang like a big firework bursting.

We stop the moped and look back. Two, three. One more. The explosions echo one after another, and halfway up the mountain—where we were just a few minutes ago—thick black smoke is rising. In slow motion, an enormous transmission tower begins tilting.

"Tesshi…!"

My voice quavers.

"Ha-ha!"

Tesshi's breath is shaky, too. It sounds like a laugh.

There's an even bigger explosion, and the lights of the town instantly go dark.

"Hey," Tesshi intones, sounding kind of dazed.

"The power's out," I say, stating the obvious.

It worked. We did it.

Suddenly, sirens well up, beginning to wail.

oooOOOOOOOOooooo…!

The earsplitting noise reverberates from speakers all over town. It's an ominous sound, like a giant's scream, and it ricochets off the mountains, pervading the area.

It's Saya. She's hijacked the wireless disaster prevention system.

We exchange wordless nods, then straddle the moped again. As we race toward the shrine, the speakers broadcasting Saya's voice spur us on. Slowly, calmly, as if her earlier tearful cries were fake, she delivers the message we came up with:

"This is Town Hall. An explosion has occurred at Itomori Substation. There is a danger of further explosions and forest fires."

Tesshi's moped goes off the prefectural road and climbs up a narrow mountain track. It's the gentler slope up to the shrine—this way, we can take the moped all the way to the back of the main building and avoid the stone stairs on the shrine approach. The seat shakes violently, and I cling to Tesshi's back as I listen to Saya's voice booming through the town. She sounds exactly like her big sister. Nobody would suspect this isn't a broadcast from the town hall.

"People in the following districts are requested to evacuate to Itomori High School immediately. Kadoiri District, Sakagami District, Miyamori District, Oyazawa District..."

"This's it. C'mon, Mitsuha!"

"Right!"

We leap off the moped and run down the set of wooden steps up the slope of the mountain behind the shrine. From between the trees, I can see the roofs of the long rows of stalls set up on the shrine grounds and the people milling around among them, like fish crowded too closely in a dark tank. As we run, we take off our helmets and throw them away.

"I repeat: This is Itomori Town Hall. An explosion has occurred at the substation. There is a danger of further explosions and forest fires..."

When we hit the bottom of the stairs, we're behind the main shrine building. The silhouettes of the people gathered for the festival are just ahead, and I hear an uneasy murmur. Tesshi and I dash into their midst as if we're racing each other, yelling.

"Ruuun! A forest fire's comin'! This place ain't safe!"

Tesshi's voice is unbelievably loud, like he's using a megaphone. I shout, too, determined not to be outdone. "Please run! There's a forest fire! Run!" We emerge in the very center of the grounds.

"Yeah, they said there really is a forest fire!"

"C'mon, let's get outta here."

"We're walkin' all the way to the high school?"

The broadcast set the evacuation in motion, and our shouts are pushing it along. Men and women in traditional wear, children, and old people holding their grandkids' hands all begin filing toward the shrine gate at the exit. I'm relieved. If things go on like this, we'll make it for sure. It's all thanks to him... "Him"?

"Mitsuha!"

Tesshi calls my name sharply. I look up at him.

"This ain't good!"

Following his gaze around us, I see lots of people sitting down and taking it easy by the stalls or standing, idly talking. They're even smoking cigarettes or drinking, chatting away and enjoying the evening.

"There's no way we're movin' all these folks unless an actual forest fire comes through! We have to get them to send out the fire brigade and direct the evacuation. You get to the town hall, and this time make sure the mayor..."

Tesshi's flustered voice is right above my head, but it sounds terribly far away... Him?

"Hey. Mitsuha? What's up?"

"...Tesshi, listen, what'll I do?"

My mind isn't working, and before I know it, I'm pleading to Tesshi.

"His name... I can't remember his name!"

Tesshi's face twists with worry. Suddenly, he yells at me. "Who the hell cares, you idiot?! Look around! You started all this!"

He's glaring at me, furious. Belatedly, I notice that Saya's call to **"Please evacuate to Itomori High School"** is now erratic, as if she's about to burst into tears.

"Mitsuha, *go*!" Tesshi gives a heartrending yell, practically begging this time. "Go talk your dad around!"

My spine straightens as though he's slapped me across the face.

"...Right!"

I nod as firmly as I can, then bolt into a sprint, trying to shake myself free.

Behind me, I hear Tesshi scream again. "I said run, y'all! Get to the high school!"

Saya's voice echoes all over town. **"There is a danger of forest fires. Please evacuate to Itomori High School."** I push my way through the lumbering crowd, under the shrine gate, down the stone stairs on the shrine approach.

"You started all this," Tesshi'd said. He's right: This is something I—we—started. Still running, I glance at the comet overhead. With the lights on the ground extinguished, the comet's even brighter. Its long tail streams over the clouds. It's scattering shining scales like a giant moth. *I'm not letting you get your way*, I think, as if challenging it to a fight.

It's all right. You'll make it.

Somebody once told me that with conviction. I repeat the words silently to myself.

✳   ✳   ✳

It was early autumn, and I was still in middle school.

I'd finally gotten used to living with just my dad, and after finishing a dinner that we'd both worked hard to make (and still hadn't been all that good), I was drinking tea and eating an apple while Dad enjoyed a beer.

That day, the news about the comet's closest approach had pretty much taken over the TV. I wasn't all that interested in stars or the cosmos, but I did find it kind of amazing how the universe is actually overflowing with phenomena that exist on a completely different scale from humans, like a solar orbit that lasts twelve hundred years or an orbital radius over 10.4 billion miles. As impressions went, it was dumb. Still, it struck me as so awesome that it made me shiver and, at the same time, so frightening it set my heart trembling as well.

"Look!"

Suddenly, the announcer who'd been delivering commentary yelled in excitement.

"The comet appears to have split in two. Around it are…what seem to be countless shooting stars."

When the camera zoomed in, the comet really had forked above the background of Tokyo skyscrapers. Thin lines like a meteor shower appeared and disappeared at its tip. There was a delicate, almost artificial beauty about it, and my eyes went wide.

✳   ✳   ✳

Abruptly, the wireless broadcast is interrupted by the click of an opening door.

I hear a short shriek from Saya, and then several familiar male voices emerge from the speakers.

"Kid, what are you doin'?!"

"Hurry, shut it off!"

There's a clatter like a chair falling over, and then the wireless broadcast cuts off with a brief burst of shrill feedback.

"Saya…!" I stop, calling her name involuntarily.

The teachers caught her. Large beads of sweat pop out as if they've just remembered their jobs, falling to the asphalt with audible drips. I'm on the road that circles around the lake, the one that goes to the town hall and the high school, and I start hearing bewildered voices from several evacuees.

"What? What's goin' on?"

"Huh? Was there some sort of trouble?"

"What about the evacuation?"

Oh no. A moment later, a voice booms from the wireless speakers again.

"This is Itomori Town Hall."

It's not Saya or her big sister. It's the middle-aged guy in charge of Town Hall broadcasts, someone I hear every once in a while.

"We are currently looking into the circumstances surrounding the accident. We request that all residents refrain from panicking. Please stay where you are and wait for further instructions."

I lurch forward again.

They figured out where the broadcast was coming from, and the town hall contacted the school. Saya's going to get grilled by the teachers. Tesshi will be in big trouble, too, if this keeps up.

"I repeat: Do not panic. Stay where you are and wait for further instructions."

They can't stay where they are! I have to make them stop this broadcast!

I leave the prefectural road, plunging from the gap in the asphalt onto a slope that's overgrown with brush. It's a shortcut to the town hall. The thorns on the bushes scrape and sting my bare legs. A spiderweb clings to my face, and little winged bugs get into my mouth.

Finally, I hit the bottom of the slope and run out onto asphalt again. I can't see anyone around me. There's only the voice from the wireless broadcast, issuing orders to stay put. As I run, I spit out the saliva that's pooled in my mouth, wiping my sweaty, tear-streaked, cobweb-sticky face with my sleeve. My legs have gone watery, and I stagger. Even then, I keep running. I'm going downhill, and I'm not losing speed. I'm on a gentle curve, and it's bringing me closer to the guardrail. Below it is the incline down to the lake.

"…Huh?!"

A feeling that something's wrong makes me look in that direction. The lake shines faintly. I strain my eyes.

No, it isn't the water glowing. Its calm surface is reflecting the sky. Like a mirror, the lake reveals two shining tails… Two? I tilt my head to the sky.

Oh, the comet— It's finally…

"…It split!"

*   *   *

I was channel surfing. Every station jabbered excitedly about the unexpected astronomy show.

"The comet has definitely split in two."

"This wasn't predicted beforehand, correct?"

"Still, what an extraordinarily fantastic sight…"

"Is it safe to conclude that the nucleus of the comet has divided?"

"The tidal forces don't seem to have surpassed the Roche limit, so it's possible that an abnormality of some kind occurred within the comet itself—"

"As of yet, the National Astronomical Observatory has issued no statement…"

"A similar case occurred in 1994, when Comet Shoemaker-Levy fell into Jupiter. On that occasion, it split into at least twenty-one fragments…"

"Do you suppose it's dangerous?"

"Comets are masses of ice, so we believe it will melt before it reaches Earth's surface. Even if it does become a meteorite, in terms of probability, the likelihood that it will fall on an inhabited area is extremely low…"

"It's difficult to predict the trajectories of the fragments in real time—"

"The fact that we're witnessing such a magnificent astronomical phenomenon, combined with the fact that it happens to be night-time in Japan, may be the sort of good fortune that comes only once in a thousand years for those of us who are alive in this era—"

"I'm gonna go look!" I told my dad.

Without even thinking about it, I jumped up from my chair and rushed down the building's stairs.

From a hill in the neighborhood, I watched the night sky.

It held innumerable sparkling lights, as if another Tokyo had been layered over the sky. It was like a scene from a dream, a view that was simply, utterly beautiful.

The comet, split in two, brings my own solitude into stark relief as I race through the blacked-out town like a lost child.

Who, who? Who is he?

Without taking my eyes off the comet, running as if I'm perpetually falling, I desperately try to think.

Someone important. Someone I can't forget. Someone I didn't want to forget.

It's not much farther to Town Hall. Not much longer until that comet becomes a meteorite.

Who? Who? Who are you?

I summon the very last of my strength and pick up speed.

—What's your name?

"Aah!" I cry out automatically.

My toe caught in a pit in the asphalt, and in the moment I realize I'm falling, the ground is already imminent. There's a shock, a blow to the face. My body tumbles limply. Stabbing pain spreads through me. My field of vision spins, and my consciousness goes black.

....
....
......But.

Your voice reaches me.

"So we don't forget each other after we wake up."

That's what you said then, and...

"Let's write down our names."

You wrote on my hand.

On the ground, I open my eyes.

My pain-blurred vision finds my clenched right hand. I open the fingers, or try to. They're stiff and wooden. Even so, little by little, I uncurl them.

There are letters there. I strain my eyes.

I love you

For a moment, I stop breathing. I try to stand. My muscles feel weak, and it takes a long time. Even so, I manage to get myself back on my feet, standing on the asphalt. Then I look at my palm one more time. All that's written there, in nostalgic handwriting I've seen somewhere before, are the words *I love you*.

...But this isn't... Tears spill over, and my vision blurs again. Something like a warm wave spreads through me, like a spring that's welled up with the tears. Still crying, I laugh, talking to you.

This doesn't tell me your name.

Then one more time, I surge forward with all my might.

I'm not afraid of anything now. I'm not scared of anyone. I'm not lonely anymore.

I finally understand.

I'm in love. We're in love.

That means we'll meet again. I'm sure of it.

And so I'll live.

I'll survive this.

No matter what happens, even if the stars fall, I will live.

✳ ✳ ✳

Right up until it happened, no one managed to predict that the comet's nucleus would shatter near Earth, or that there was a huge rocky mass buried in its ice-covered core.

The town happened to be holding its autumn festival that day. The strike occurred at 8:42 PM. The point of impact was near Miyamizu Shrine, where the festival was being held.

The meteorite instantly destroyed a wide area, centered on the shrine. The crater formed by the impact was nearly half a mile across. Water from the lake beside it rushed in, swallowing the remains of the town. Itomori became the site of the worst meteorite disaster in human history.

I remember these things as I look down over gourd-shaped New Itomori Lake. It reflects the sun in the midst of a faint morning haze, endlessly serene. It's hard to imagine that three years ago it was the site of such a tragedy. I can't quite believe that the comet I saw in the sky over Tokyo did *this*.

I'm standing on a rock-littered mountain peak, all alone.

I was here when I woke up.

For no real reason, I look at my right hand. There's a single, half-drawn line on my palm.

"What is this...?" I mutter quietly.

"What was I doing way out here?"

Chapter Eight

Your Name.

I have a few habits I've unconsciously picked up.

For example, when I'm feeling rushed and flustered, I touch the back of my neck. When I wash my face, I look into my eyes, reflected in the mirror. Even on mornings when I'm in a hurry, when I step out the front door, I pause and take a long look at the scenery.

I also gaze at my palm for no reason.

"The next station is…Yoyogi…Yoyogi."

As the synthetic audio announces the station, I realize I'm doing it again. I look away from my right hand, gazing absently out the window instead. We're slowing down, and beyond the glass, the crowd of people standing on the platform flows by.

Abruptly, my whole body breaks out in goose bumps.

A beat later, I think, *It's her.*

She was standing on the platform.

The train stops. Even waiting for the doors to open seems to take too long, and I leave the train at a sprint. I turn in a circle, scanning the platform. Several passengers dart suspicious glances at me as they pass, and my head finally cools down.

I'm not looking for anyone in particular. "She" isn't anybody.

This is yet another habit I've picked up unawares, and it's probably a weird one.

The next thing I know, still standing on the platform, I'm gazing at my palm again. *Just a little more*, I think.

Just a little longer. Just a little more.

I don't know what wish accompanies those words, but somewhere along the way, I've started longing for it.

"I applied to your company because I like buildings— Or, no...I mean cityscapes. The landscape of people living their lives in general."

The faces of the four interviewers in front of me cloud slightly. *No, no, that's just my imagination*, I think. This is the first time I've managed to make it to the second round of interviews at a company. *I can't blow this chance*, I think, psyching myself up again.

"I always have. Even I don't really understand why, but, um... Anyway, I like them. What I mean is, I like watching buildings and the people who live and work there. That's why I often go to cafés and restaurants. I even worked at a few part-time—"

"I see." One of the interviewers cuts me off gently. "Then could you tell us why you chose to enter the construction field, rather than the restaurant industry?"

She's a middle-aged woman, the only one of the four who looked kind, and I finally realize I've been blabbing about an irrelevant reason for applying. I break out in a sweat in a suit I'm not yet used to wearing.

"Well, I... Serving customers at my part-time job was fun, but I guess you could say I wanted to be involved in something bigger..."

Something bigger? That's a middle school answer. Even I can tell my face is flushing red.

"I mean... The way I see it, there's no telling when even Tokyo could disappear."

This time, the interviewers' faces really do cloud over. Realizing

I've been touching the back of my neck, I hastily put hands on my knees again.

"So if it does— No, precisely because it will someday, I want to create the sort of town that warms people, even if it's only a memory—"

Agh, it's no good. Even I can't follow what I'm saying. I've failed this one, too. Thinking this, I glance at the gray skyscrapers that tower behind the interviewers, and I feel like crying.

"So? How many companies have you interviewed at, including today?" Takagi asks me.

"I'm not keeping track," I tell him glumly.

Looking awfully entertained, Tsukasa says, "I don't think you're going to make it."

"I don't want to hear that from you," I cut back crossly.

"Sure it's not because you just don't look good in a suit?" Takagi grins.

"You guys aren't much different!" I bristle angrily.

"I've got unofficial offers from two companies," he counters cheerfully.

"I have eight," Tsukasa condescends.

"Rrgh…!"

I have no comeback. My coffee cup rattles in my fingers as they tremble with humiliation.

Tweedle.

My phone chirps from the table. I check the message, drain what's left of my coffee in one gulp, and stand.

Come to think of it, the three of us came to this café a lot when we were in high school. The memory strikes me after I've waved good-bye to Tsukasa and Takagi and started jogging toward the station. Life was so carefree back then. I didn't have to think about the future or finding a job, and somehow, every day was ludicrously fun. Especially that one summer—I think it was during my second year of high school. It seems like that summer was especially thrilling. What happened that year? I think back and conclude there wasn't anything in particular. I guess I must've just been at an age when absolutely anything was enough to trigger a giggling fit.

…Wait, no, that's something they say about girls… Absentmindedly, I hop down the stairs to the subway.

"Ooh. Job hunting, hmm?"

Okudera-senpai looks up from her phone, sees me in my suit, and smiles. It's evening, and the area in front of Yotsuya Station is filled with the faintly languid hum of people released from their days at work or school.

"Ha-ha. Well, it's not going so great."

"Hmm…" Okudera-senpai murmurs, bringing her face closer to mine. She inspects me from head to toe with a frown. Then, gravely, she asks, "You don't think it's because suits don't look good on you?"

"I-is it really that bad?!" Involuntarily, I look down at myself.

"Oh, come on, I'm joking!"

Okudera-senpai beams, her expression changing easily.

"Let's walk a little," Okudera-senpai says, and I follow her. We set off, going against the current of the university students on Shinjuku Street. We cut across Kioicho, then cross the Benkei Bridge. For the first time, I realize that the trees lining the roads are changing color. About half the people we pass have on lightweight coats. Okudera-senpai is wearing a loose ash-gray jacket, too.

"What's going on today? Your text came out of the blue."

Feeling as if I'm the only one who hasn't kept up with the season, I turn to Okudera-senpai beside me.

"What?" Her glossy lips pout. "I can't get in touch with you without a reason?"

"No, no, no!" I wave my hands hastily.

"You're happy to see me, aren't you? It's been a long time."

"Y-yes. I am."

She smiles in satisfaction at my answer, then continues. "I was in the area for work and thought I'd like to see your face, Taki." She was hired by a major clothing chain and works at a branch store in Chiba now. "Life in the suburbs is fun, too, but Tokyo really is lively and one of a kind," she tells me, gazing at her surroundings like she's a little awestruck. "Look," she says suddenly, and I raise my head.

We're crossing a pedestrian bridge, so we're eye level with the giant outdoor display screen above an electronics store. It's showing aerial footage of gourd-shaped Itomori Lake and the words *The Comet Disaster—Eight Years Later* in big letters.

"We went to Itomori once, didn't we?" Okudera-senpai narrows her eyes, as though she's searching distant memories. "You were still in high school, Taki, so it must've been…"

"Five years ago, maybe?" I finish the sentence for her.

"That long…" She exhales a little, as if surprised. "I'm forgetting all sorts of things."

She's right, I think. As we come down off the pedestrian bridge and walk up Sotobori Street where it runs along the edge of the Akasaka Estate lands, I try remembering that day.

It was the summer of my second year in high school— No, it was just about this time of year, early autumn. Tsukasa, Okudera-senpai, and I went on a short trip. We transferred from the Shinkansen to an express train, went all the way to Gifu, and wandered aimlessly around the area along the local train line. Right, and we went into this ramen shop that was standing all by itself on the side of the national highway. And then… From that point on, my memories blur and grow distant, as if belonging to a past life. Maybe we fought? I have a vague recollection of leaving the other two and going off on my own. I climbed a mountain somewhere all alone, spent the night there, and then went back to Tokyo by myself the next day.

That's right... Back then, I was obsessed with the events surrounding that comet.

In the sort of natural disaster that's happened only a few times in human history, a fragment of the comet destroyed a town. And yet, in spite of that, almost all the town's residents survived. It was a miraculous night. The day the comet fell, Itomori just happened to be holding a town-wide disaster drill, and most of the locals had already been evacuated from the area impacted.

It was such a huge coincidence and such incredible luck, that there were all sorts of whispered rumors after the disaster. The unprecedented astronomical phenomenon and the townspeople's stupendous luck were enough to stir up the media's and public's imagination. All sorts of irresponsible ideas flew around wildly for days on end, from folklore-type stories that linked the comet's visit with Itomori's dragon-god legend, to political statements that either praised or questioned the mayor of Itomori's use of plenary power in forcing an evacuation, to occult rumors that the meteorite strike had actually been foretold. Other strange details, such as the fact that the town had been so isolated it was practically a landlocked desert island, and the fact that the power across the entire area had gone out about two hours before the meteorite strike, spurred public speculation. Society's excitement lasted until the programs to resettle the victims in other areas had calmed down a bit, but as with most incidents, just about the time the seasons changed, the topic of Itomori slowly disappeared from public conversation.

Still... Once again, it strikes me as strange. I'd even drawn sketches of Itomori, several of them. Not only that, but my feverish interest had materialized unexpectedly, a few years after the comet strike. *Something* had visited me suddenly, like a delayed comet itself, then vanished without a trace. What in the world had it been?

Well, I guess it's not important, I think, watching the streets of Yotsuya sink into the dusk from a hill beside Sotobori Street. It really doesn't matter now. I write the thought on a wall in my mind. I need to be focusing on finding a job next year, not ancient history I don't really remember.

"The wind's come up," Okudera-senpai whispers, and her long, wavy hair rises softly. A sweet scent I smelled once, somewhere long ago and far away, reaches my nose faintly. Like a conditioned reflex, the fragrance sparks a melancholy inside me.

"Thanks for spending the day with me. This is far enough," Okudera-senpai says when I offer to see her to the turnstile at the station.

We ate dinner at the Italian restaurant where we'd worked part-time as students. Thanks to a promise I totally don't remember making—"Come to think of it, Taki, didn't you say you'd treat me after you graduated from high school?"—I ended up paying for Okudera-senpai. Even so, I felt a little bit proud picking up the check.

"You know, I had no idea the place we used to work had such good food."

"Yeah, all the meals they gave us during our shifts were like school lunches."

"We went for years without catching on."

We laugh. Okudera-senpai draws a deep, contented breath, then says, "All right. I'll see you later." She waves at me, and there's a band like a thin drop of water shining on her ring finger.

"You'll find happiness someday, too," she'd assured me earlier over an espresso, after informing me she was getting married. I couldn't manage a good response—I just mumbled something congratulatory.

I'm not particularly unhappy, I think, watching Okudera-senpai's silhouette descend the pedestrian-bridge stairs. That said, I don't really understand what happiness is yet, either.

I abruptly inspect my palm. All that's there is an absence.

Just a little longer…, I think one more time.

*   *   *

Before I know it, the season's changed again.

An unusually typhoon-filled autumn passed, moving straight into a winter of nothing but cold rain. Tonight, too, the rain is whispering down unabated, like the memory of a pleasant chat on some bygone day. Christmas lights twinkle beyond windows beaded thickly with water droplets.

I take a sip from my paper cup of coffee, as if swallowing my scattered thoughts, then look down at my notebook again. Even now, in December, it's packed with job-hunting appointments.

Visits with former upperclassmen to discuss their work, information sessions, entry deadlines, paper schedules, interview dates. The range is chaotic, covering everything from major general contractors to design offices to old-town factories, and as I check the notebook against the schedule on my phone, even I'm a bit disgusted by it. I start organizing the main points from tomorrow onward, writing them into my notebook.

"Y'know, I'd like to go to at least one more bridal fair."

Mixed with the sound of the rain, the conversations of strangers sound a bit like secrets. The couple behind me has been discussing their wedding for a while now, and it makes me think of Okudera-senpai. Their voices and bearing are completely different, though. There's a bit of an easygoing regional accent to their speech, and their conversation seems completely relaxed, as if they're childhood friends. I'm not really listening, but my ears pick up what they're saying.

"Again?" The guy sounds annoyed, but even then, there's no mistaking the affection in his tone. "We've been to a ton of fairs already. They were all pretty much the same stuff."

"Well, I was thinkin' a Shinto ceremony might be nice, too."

"You said your dream was to have it in a chapel."

"This is a once-in-a-lifetime thing. I can't make up my mind that easily."

"But you said you did make up your mind," the guy quietly complains, and I chuckle.

The girl ignores him. "Hmm...," she murmurs, thinking. "Never mind that. Tesshi, you gotta shave off those whiskers before the ceremony."

I was about to drink my coffee, but my hand stops dead.

My pulse is speeding up, though I don't understand why.

"I'll lose a few pounds for you, 'kay?"

"But you're eatin' cake!"

"I'll start for real tomorrow!"

Slowly, I look behind me.

The two of them have already gotten up from their chairs and are pulling on their coats. The tall, skinny guy is wearing a stocking cap over his buzzed head. I just catch a glimpse of his profile. The girl is petite, and her bobbed hair makes her seem young, almost like a student. The pair turns away and leaves the café. For some reason, I can't take my eyes off their backs.

"Thank you for your visit." The café employee's voice reaches my ears indistinctly, mingled with the rain.

By the time I leave the café, the rain has turned to snow.

Maybe it's because of all the moisture up in the atmosphere, but the town is oddly warm in the falling snow. I feel strangely uneasy, as if I've wandered into the wrong season. It seems to me as if each and every person I pass is hiding some important secret, and in spite of myself, I keep turning back to look at them.

I go straight to the ward library, which is almost ready to close for the evening. The sparseness of the handful of readers in the vast, vaulted space makes the air inside feel even chillier than outside. I take a seat and open the book I've retrieved from the stacks. The title is *Vanished Itomori—Complete Records*. It's a collection of photographs.

As if removing an ancient seal, I slowly page through the book.

Gingko trees and an elementary school. The shrine's steep stairs, with their view over the lake. A shrine gate with peeling paint. A tiny railroad crossing, like toy building blocks abruptly set down in the fields. A pointlessly expansive parking lot, two snack bars right next to each other, a drab concrete high school. A prefectural road with old, cracked asphalt. A guardrail that traces a winding hill road. Vinyl greenhouses, reflecting the sky.

They're the sort of ordinary sights you see all over Japan, so I recognize all of them. I can visualize the temperature of the stone walls and the chill of the wind, just as if I'd lived there.

Why is this so…? I wonder as I turn the pages.

Why do the unremarkable sights of a town that no longer exists make my heart hurt this much?

Once, fueled by intense emotions, I made some sort of resolution.

I remember this out of nowhere when I look up at the light in somebody's window on my way home, or when I reach for a box lunch in the convenience store, or when I retie my loose shoelaces.

I decided something once. I took an oath because I met somebody—no, so that I would meet somebody.

Washing my face and staring into the mirror, tossing a plastic bag in the trash, squinting at the morning sun between the buildings, I think this and smile wryly.

"Somebody," "something." In the end, I don't know a thing.

Still, I think as I close the door at an interview.

Still, even now, I'm fighting my way through. Perhaps it's a bit dramatic to say, but I'm struggling against life. Wasn't that what I decided once? To struggle. To live. To breathe and walk. To run. To eat. To bind, *musubi*. To live an ordinary life so I shed tears over the sights of a perfectly ordinary town.

Just a little longer, I think.

Just a little is fine. Just a little more.

I don't know what it is I want, but I keep on wishing for something.

Just a little longer. Just a little more.

The cherry blossoms bloom and scatter, long rains wash the streets, white clouds billow high, the leaves change color, freezing winds blow. Then the cherry trees bloom again.

The days are accelerating.

I've graduated from university, and I'm working at the job I somehow managed to find. I spend every day with the desperation of a man trying not to be flung from a careening vehicle. There are times when I can believe I'm getting closer, in very tiny increments, to the place I want to be.

In the morning, when I wake up, I stare at my right hand. There are little drops of water on my index finger. By the time I notice them, both the dream I was in a moment earlier and the tears that for an instant stained my eyes have evaporated.

Just a little longer. With that thought, I get out of bed.

Just a little longer.

As I recite the wish, I face the mirror and tie my hair cord. I pull my arms through the sleeves of my spring suit. I open the door of my apartment and, for a moment, gaze at the Tokyo cityscape that unfurls before me. I climb the station stairs, go through the automated turnstile, and board a packed commuter train. The little patch of blue sky I can see beyond the heads of the crowd is piercingly clear.

I lean against the train door, looking out. The city teems with people, in the windows of buildings, in cars, on pedestrian bridges. A hundred people to a car, a thousand people to a train, a thousand trains crisscrossing the city. Gazing at them, I make my wish. Just a little longer.

In that instant, with absolutely no warning, I see her.

And then, I see him.

He's there, close enough to touch if it weren't for the window-panes, on a train running parallel to this one. He's looking straight at me, and his eyes are wide with surprise, like mine. Then I realize what the wish I've carried for so long really is.

She's there, just a few feet away. I don't even know her name, but I know it's her. Our trains are pulling away from each other. Then another train passes between us, and I lose sight of her.

But I finally know what I'm wishing for.

I wanted to stay with her, just a little longer.
I want to be with him, just a little more.

The train stops, and I dash through the streets. I'm looking for her. I'm already positive she's looking for me, too.

We've met before. Or, no, that could be my imagination. It might be just an assumption, something like a dream. It might be a delusion, like past lives. Even so, I—we—wanted to stay together a little longer. We want to be together, just a little more.

As I run along the sloping road, I wonder, *Why am I running? Why am I searching?* I probably know the answer. I don't remember it, but everything in my body knows. I turn at a narrow alley, and the road drops off. Stairs. I walk over to them, look down…and there he is.

Fighting back the urge to run, I climb the stairs slowly. A wind that smells like flowers lifts my suit jacket and fills it out into a bell.

She's standing at the top of the stairs, but I can't look at her directly. I only watch her out of the corner of my eye. She's descending the stairs. The click of her shoes drifts softly into the spring air. My heart is leaping in my rib cage.

As we approach each other, we keep our eyes downcast. He doesn't say anything. I can't say anything, either. Then, still without speaking, we pass each other. In that moment, I feel a tense, squeezing pain all over, as though something inside me has taken hold of my heart. *This is wrong*, I think fiercely. We can't possibly be strangers. It goes against something as basic as the mechanics of the universe, or the laws of life. And so…

And so I turn around. She turns, too, with the exact same speed. She's standing on the stairs, the streets of Tokyo behind her, her eyes wide and round. I realize her long hair is tied back with a cord the color of the evening sun. My whole body trembles slightly.

I finally found him. We finally met. Just as I think I'll probably burst into tears unless I do something, I realize I'm already crying. Seeing this, he smiles. Even as I cry, I smile, too. The spring air carries with it all sorts of apprehension and anticipation, and I draw a deep breath.

Then we open our mouths at the same time.

Like children who've agreed to go on the count of three, we say together:

What's your name?

Afterword

To be honest, I didn't intend to write this novel.

It may be rude to the readers for me to say something like that, but I thought *your name.* worked best as an animated film.

This book, *your name.*, is the novel version of an animated movie I directed, which is scheduled to open in the summer of 2016. In other words, it's a novelization of the movie, but actually, as I'm writing this afterword, the movie hasn't been finished yet. They tell me it will take another three months or so to complete. That means the novel will go out into the world first, so if you asked me which is the original work, the movie or the novel, I'd have to say, "It's complicated." Writing this book has altered some of my personal impressions as well. For example, *Mitsuha was a pretty laid-back, optimistic kid, wasn't she?* and *Taki really is hopeless with women.* It's likely to influence the postrecording (when the actors and voice actors create the voices for us) for the movie. This "gift exchange" between a movie and a novel was a first for me, and to tell the truth, it was a lot of fun.

There are no major differences between the novel and the movie as far as the story is concerned, but there are slight differences in the way it's told. The novel is written from Taki's and Mitsuha's first-person perspectives; in other words, from their viewpoints only. They can't tell us about things they don't know. Meanwhile, movies generally use third-person perspectives: the world as the camera shows it to us. For that reason, many scenes are literally told from a high-angle viewpoint and include characters other than Taki and Mitsuha. I think it's more than possible to enjoy either work on its own, but due to the unique characteristics of each medium, they inevitably complement each other.

I wrote the novel on my own, but movies are made by the hands of many people. The script for *your name.* took shape over several months of preliminary meetings with the Toei (the movie company) *your name.* team. Producer Genki Kawamura's suggestions were always brisk and decisive, and although I sometimes secretly thought, *He's really superficial* (because he's the sort of person who says even important things like they don't mean much), he always showed me the way.

In addition, I wrote this book both at home and in the movie production studio, about half in each location, and I think it's thanks to the animation director, Masashi Ando, that I managed to complete it. It wasn't that I discussed the novel with him. It's just that, thanks to his truly dedicated work on the movie itself, I was able to relax even in the pandemonium of an animated film production site and make time to work on the book.

Then there's the score by RADWIMPS, the group in charge of the movie's music. Naturally, there's no background music in the novel, but the book was greatly influenced by the world of RADWIMPS's lyrics. The role music plays in the *your name.* movie is a big one, and I hope you'll pay particular attention to how it was rendered in both the movie and the novel. (In order to do that, I guess you'll need to see the movie. Please do go see it!)

I wrote in the beginning that I thought this story worked best as an animated film, but that's because the movie is—as I mentioned before—a splendid crystallization of the talents of many people. I think movies are in a place that's far beyond the ability of individuals.

Even so, in the end, I did write a novel version.

At some point, I changed my mind, and I began wanting to write it.

I had the feeling that, somewhere, there were boys and girls like Taki and Mitsuha. This story is a fantasy, of course, but I do think there are people somewhere who've had experiences similar to theirs, and who hold similar feelings inside. People who've lost precious loved ones or places, and who've privately decided to "struggle and fight," even so. People who believe that they're sure to find something someday, even though it hasn't happened yet, and who keep reaching out for it. I felt that those feelings needed to be related with an immediacy that differed from the glamour of the movie, and I think that's why I wrote this book.

Thank you very much for picking it up, and for reading it.

March 2016, Makoto Shinkai

Essay

GENKI KAWAMURA

"Please write the essay."

That's what Makoto Shinkai said to me in a meeting room at CoMix Wave Films.

The sudden request flustered me, and I told him I thought interpretive essays should be written objectively, by third parties.

I'm the producer of the *your name.* movie, and I don't have that perspective anymore.

Even so, Shinkai wouldn't back down. He pressed me. *Please. I want you to do this, no matter what.*

Several months later, I read the novel. It was a wonderful book.

At that point, I thought I understood why Shinkai had asked me for the essay.

He didn't want me to "interpret" anything, I realized. He wanted somebody who was "in the family" to reveal how this novel came to be.

Two years ago, I decided to make a feature film with Makoto Shinkai.

That night, I was drinking sake with him at a cheap pub under the elevated tracks in Yurakucho.

We were talking, me with a highball, him with a draft beer.

Voices of a Distant Star. The Place Promised in Our Early Days. 5 Centimeters Per Second.

Shinkai writes love stories about boys and girls who pass each other by in beautiful, magnificent worlds. I told him I wanted him to make his newest work "Makoto Shinkai's best film."

I wanted people who didn't yet know Shinkai to encounter his world and be astonished (the way I was floored when I saw *Voices of a Distant Star* fourteen years ago). I also wanted people who had kept up with Shinkai's works to witness, as if for the first time, what this particular talent could accomplish.

In addition, I told him I wanted the new work to be endlessly musical. (Makoto Shinkai's works always have splendid music.) I asked him if there were any musicians he liked, and he named a certain band. I'd been on friendly terms with that band's front man for a while, and under the influence of drink, I sent him a text.

"I started looking for you in your third life back."

. Half a year later, Yojiro Noda of RADWIMPS sent over a demo of "Third Life Back," the theme song. It was a fantastic track that will probably turn out to be epoch-making for RADWIMPS as well.

"I'm so psyched that I'm out in a downpour getting soaked as I listen to it."

For some reason, that Line message from Shinkai almost made me cry.

In this world, which is overflowing with encounters, it's hard to find your soul mate. Even if you do find them, who's going to prove to you that they really are your soul mate?

Makoto Shinkai and Yojiro Noda wrote the story of a pair who keep missing each other in an endlessly big world.

These two met as if guided by fate, and the result was a miraculous collaboration (even if it was triggered by a pub under the train tracks).

Makoto Shinkai wrote the story and script, Yojiro Noda picked them up and expanded them as music, and together, they became this book. In addition, although the movie is nearly finished, because this book was written, it's filling out even more. Seriously, how was this production so lucky?

"I'm not going to write a novel this time."

That's what Shinkai said, but Yojiro Noda's music made him write it.

It's not possible to play audio in novels, but I can hear RAD-WIMPS's songs from this one.

I think it's a rare book, the product of a fateful encounter.

In 2012, I wrote a novel called *If Cats Disappeared from the World*.

It was a portrait of a dying postman.

I thought I was writing about death, but at some point, it turned into a story about memories.

What is the cruelest thing, as far as people are concerned? Death, naturally. That's what I always thought.

However, there's something that's crueler than death.

It's forgetting the person you love while you're alive.

Where do human memories live?

Are they in the synaptic circuitry of the brain? Do retinas and fingertips hold memories, too? Or is there an invisible, amorphous, mistlike, spiritual collective somewhere, and that's where the memories reside? Something we'd call the heart or the mind or the soul. Is it something you can take out and stick back in, like a memory card with an OS on it?

In the book, Taki wonders to himself about this.

Humans are mysterious creatures. We forget the important things, and all we remember are the things that don't matter. Unlike memory cards, we don't have the ability to keep the important stuff and delete what we don't need. I always wondered why that was.

However, now that I've read this book, I feel as if I understand, just a little.

People forget the important things.

That said, by resisting, by struggling against that, they gain life.

your name., a movie that tells the love story of a boy and girl "struggling, magnificently" in this cruel world, will be completed very shortly. Without a doubt, it's going to be "Makoto Shinkai's best film"— No, let me rephrase that. The world is about to meet "Makoto Shinkai's ultimate masterpiece."

Now, with the same feelings as the people who've read this novel, I'm looking forward to my encounter with that movie from the bottom of my heart.

(Film producer and novelist)

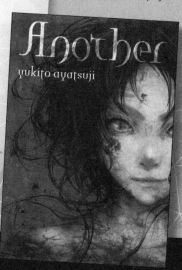